D1045226

INNER SANCTUM MYSTERY   AN INNER SANCTUM

PORTRAIT
OF A
DEAD
HEIRESS

AN INNER SANCTUM MYSTERY

BY

Thomas B. Dewey

SIMON AND SCHUSTER · NEW YORK

Library of Congress Catalog Card Number: 65-18653
Manufactured in the United States of America
By Vail-Ballou Press, Inc., Binghamton, N.Y.

PORTRAIT
OF A
DEAD
HEIRESS

I

WHEN LORRIE KING, twenty-six, reached an ending, she filled the bathtub, took a large dose of Seconal, climbed into the tub and slashed her wrists. Needless to say, she died—of drowning.

That was on October 14, on a wet, windy midnight. She was discovered early in the morning of October 15 by a maid. In midafternoon of the fifteenth, a man sat across my own desk from me and talked about Lorrie King. He talked in the halting, forced way a man talks about a recent personal horror, as if he had a prickly pear stuck in his throat.

He was a doctor named Peter Kramm, a gynecologist-obstetrician, in his mid-forties, with a blocklike, not unpleasant face, and in good condition, except for the trouble in his throat.

Outside the storm had passed and there were now and then flashes of pale sunshine. It was Sunday and the street was quiet. Also it was cold, and the cold pervaded my office, which is in an old, drafty building. I had made coffee, and after a while I got up and found a brandy bottle, half full, and we added it little by little to the coffee.

"It was typical of Lorrie," he said, "not to want to make a mess. Everything down the drain."

I had no idea why he had come to me.

"You were her doctor?" I asked.

"I was her doctor and her lover."

"I see."

7

"We would have been married in three or four months. I left home a year ago."

He used some of the needled coffee as a medicine for his throat.

"Was Miss King in good health?" I asked.

"Perfect health, physically. Obviously not in her mind."

I kept quiet. It was out of my field.

"She wasn't pregnant," he said. "Even if she had been —not enough reason." Pretty soon he said, "I had enough elementary psychiatry to know that suicide doesn't happen in a passing mood. But I know damn well the act has got to be triggered."

I nodded absently.

"That's why I'm here," he said.

I looked at him then.

"Somebody drove her to it," he said. "I want to know who."

The cold settled around me. I reached for the bottle, hesitated, then pushed it out of reach.

"Oh?" I said. "Why?"

He took some more of the medicine. When he spoke, his voice was quiet and level, as if new thoughts had dissolved the obstruction.

"I loved her," he said. "For her worth and freshness and vitality. And I guess, too, because it was flattering when she began to love me in return. You see—you would have to know her as I did—she had a mind like a rapier, a gentle, feminine rapier; but she was playful, too, when it was appropriate, with originality, verve. She had the self-assurance of a wealthy girl who knows the

8

real value of money and her own real worth. She was—"

His head dropped forward.

"I'm sorry," he said, "to go on like that. Somebody drove her to this. I have to know who."

The trouble had come back to his throat. I hoped he wouldn't break down. I wasn't sure I could handle a man like that in a breakdown.

"You must have known her quite well," I said. "Surely you would know whether there was someone in her life who would—drive her to it."

He shook his head.

"No. . . . We weren't living together. She had this apartment, near here. She was fiercely independent. I loved her for that, too. But the thing is, she had some secrets. There was more in her life than I knew. She was still worrying over the decision about us. We had an agreement that I would have no permanent strings on her; that if we should marry, it would be open, subject to change. I loved her that way—I'd have made any terms, any at all."

He looked at me, square and level across the desk, and I felt that chill again.

"I loved her so much," he said firmly, "that if I weren't here now, talking to you, I would be going the way she went. Right now, this minute, you are my only link with life."

This time I picked up the bottle and poured a generous measure into my lukewarm coffee.

"You're asking me to save your life," I said. "That's a big one."

9

"I can't help it," he said. "I have got to know who made her kill herself. I don't care if it costs a million dollars—and I've got almost that much and I can get that much if I have to."

"Suppose we find out," I said. "What then? What will you do about it?"

He looked into his cup.

"I'll cross that bridge when I come to it," he said.

"Where did she get the Seconal?" I asked.

"From me," he said.

"On prescription?"

"Of course. She might have persuaded some pharmacist to increase the dose—but she didn't die of Seconal. She drowned."

"Are you satisfied with the autopsy?"

"It was done by a friend of mine. I trust his judgment."

"He didn't know about your attachment to Miss King?"

"No."

"How did she get along with her parents?"

"Her father is dead. Her mother wasn't exactly—kind to her, but she was dutiful. She didn't give her a bad time that I know of. She's up in society. Anyway, by the time I knew her, Lorrie was completely independent of her family, every way, not only financially."

I tried to think of some more questions. I had no plan to undertake the investigation, and I wasn't trying in an organized way to learn anything from him. But he had had enough confidence in me to seek me out, and he obviously needed a listener. The least I could do was to go along with him. I think that what was in the back of my mind was that if I could keep him talking and hit enough different angles, he would give up the whole idea.

"When you first met her," I asked him, "was it professionally?"

"Yes. She came in on an appointment, had a minor symptom—cervical tumor. Not serious, but it worried her. That was three years ago. At the time, she was engaged to be married. I gave her a general examination and we removed the tumor. She was in the hospital overnight. That was it."

"You know the name of the man she was to marry?"

"No. I never did."

"She was in society. Unless it was some secret, spur-of-the-moment thing, it would be in the papers, wouldn't it?"

"I suppose so. At that time, of course, it didn't mean anything to me."

"When did it begin to mean something to you?"

"Six months later. She came back. She had this recurring menstrual difficulty, even less serious than the tumor, but it was worrisome. We got to talking. She told me her marrige had not come off. There was absolutely nothing in the way of a come-on. It developed that we had a mutual interest in painting. She had painted herself, and I had fooled around at it. She had been to Paris recently, as I never had, and she talked about that. It ended in my asking her to lunch.

"A week later, on my day off, we met by arrangement at the Art Institute and spent the afternoon there. And that was about the time it hit me. It hit me hard; it sneaked up on me. She was so easy to know, so relaxed. There was nothing going on except talk, communication. Neither of us said anything about attachments. As far as I knew, she didn't have any. We met only for lunch, occasionally. I knew I was falling for her, but it was gentle, gradual, the way you come to love a picture, a scene."

He broke off and put his face in his hands.

"Oh, God," he said. "I'm sorry—I just can't seem to stop—"

"I understand," I said. "Can you tell me this? When you first saw her, examined her—"

It was my turn to break off. But I had misjudged him. The professional stuff he could handle all right. I guess you would learn that.

"What?" he asked.

"I was wondering—about her condition. Was she all right? Any signs of previous trouble, mistreatment?"

"No," he said. "She was in good health. I asked her as a matter of routine whether she had ever been married. That's a professional euphemism. She said no. I could tell she had never been pregnant."

"I see," I said. "And so then you were seeing each other for about three months."

"Yes. Now and then I would get her something—we went to auctions, commercial galleries. I bought her three pictures over a period of time. A Gauguin, I remember, a Fletcher Martin, and a Renoir—small, not too expensive pictures. She accepted them with that same frank pleasure—the way she accepted life itself. There was no strain, no coyness."

I waited, and after a moment he went on.

"Then we broke up—because I couldn't contain it any longer; I had to tell her. It was our first date for dinner. 'I love you,' I said. She took it in that same calm way she had, but she said, 'I'm flattered, but I'm not in love with you. I like you very much. I like being with you.' And she brought about, somehow, one of those agreements—that if it was getting too difficult for me, maybe we ought not to see each other any more.

"But now, with the challenge, I was all the way gone and I couldn't stay away from her. I was desperate for her, for things to go on just as before, asking nothing."

"You didn't have any resentment," I asked, "because you had been attentive, had given her gifts?"

"No, no!" he said. "It wasn't, you see, that I needed—just a girl! It was she, herself, as much of her as I could have."

"So you started seeing her again?"

"Yes, after a couple of weeks; we picked up where we had left off. But now she was wary, a little tighter than before. But she was so kind, so feminine, she never asked questions. My marriage had been going from bad to worse for some time. The preoccupation hadn't helped any, of course, but Lorrie—" he gagged, cleared his throat, and apologized, as if the mere mention of her name had brought back all the pain— "Lorrie was in no way responsible for what happened to my marriage."

Of course not, I thought. Still, she existed.

13

"Did your wife ever know of your affair with Lorrie?" I asked.

"I doubt it. Our names were never linked publicly. We didn't see other people. We stayed away from our friends when we were together. I wanted everything clean and unspoiled."

Clean and unspoiled, I thought. Do it in the bathtub. Everything down the drain.

I got up and looked out the window. There was nothing to see until a woman in a mink coat passed, walking a black poodle with a pink ribbon around its neck.

What will I do about him? I thought.

"When have you had anything to eat lately?" I asked.

He ran his hand over his face and shook his head.

"I don't know—nothing today."

"Maybe it's about time."

"How could I eat anything—?"

I was getting a little impatient.

"Could you try?" I said.

That jerked him up some.

"I guess so," he said. "Whatever you say."

Brother, I thought, with all due respect to the bereaved, you got to start getting reglued.

2

I took him across the street to Tony's joint, where you can get a good ham sandwich and where the waitress will converse or keep quiet according to your mood. The girl on duty this Sunday afternoon was a Greek named Pauline. She didn't let me down. My mood plainly said, "For God's sake, talk!"

"I'm getting married again," she said, while she arranged her setups. "Unless the guy finks out, which he might."

"Who's the guy?" I asked.

"A bartender named Hank. I don't really like him much, but he's steady. He doesn't drink or gamble, and when he's off he likes to stay home—he says."

"Why would he fink out on you?"

"Well— What are you having?"

"A ham sandwich for me, with beer," I said. "The doctor will have—?"

"Oh—the same," he said. "And could I have a double bourbon on the rocks?"

"Sure," Pauline said.

"You have the day off tomorrow?" I asked.

"No," he said, "but I don't have any deliveries and no surgery."

"It's all right with me," I said.

Pauline came back with the bourbon and two glasses of beer.

"The reason he might fink out," she said, "he's got this sports car. I guess it's a regular dream wagon. He's in love with it. I hate sports cars. I hate them to drive, to ride in and even to look at. I wouldn't think of making him get rid of it, naturally, anyway not for a few months. But he happens to know my general feelings. Sometimes he gets this look, like a guy in love with a dog, you know? 'Love me, love that car, baby, or nothing.' I hate that lousy car."

Dr. Kramm was taking some notice of her.

"If you don't like him," he said, "and you hate the car—why do you want to marry him?"

She leaned against the side of the booth—my side —and went into a kind of trance.

"It's like this," she said. "Before, I was married to this bum—a Greek. I say bum, I don't mean he didn't take care of me finance-wise. But he had the habits of a bum, a rat. This Hank the bartender is Irish. He's got respect for me. That's why."

"I see," Dr. Kramm said.

Pretty soon she came with the sandwiches.

"You a real doctor?" she asked him. "Medical, I mean?"

"Yes," he said.

"What—uh—branch?"

"Specialty?" he said. "Gynecology and obstetrics." She stared at him.

"I specialize in female diseases and deliver babies."

"Oh," she said. "That's a good combination, huh?"

"Inevitable," he said. "What's your problem?"

"Me? Oh, I don't have any problems of that nature."
She retreated behind the bar.

"I've got a patient like her," Dr. Kramm said. "My favorite patient. She has six kids now and the seventh is on the way. Came in last month and she was lying there and she said, 'It's getting to be a drag, Doctor. How can I quit?' I told her about the only sure way. 'You mean you can *fix* me?' she said. 'Like a dog or something?' I explained that I could but that I wouldn't like to. 'I should hope not,' she said. 'Because, you know, something might happen to this guy, and I might—after a while—be with some other guy and I might change my mind.' 'Exactly,' I said. So the last I heard, she has decided to relax and have the baby and probably a couple more before she quits."

It was nice to hear him talking about something besides his dead love. Pauline came back with two more glasses of beer. The doctor had finished his bourbon, and he picked up the glass, started to hand it to her, then set it down, shaking his head. Pauline lingered.

"Listen," she said, "could I ask you a question?"

"Certainly," he said.

She looked at me. I picked up my sandwich and glass of beer and got up.

"All right," I said. "Remember me on the kickback, huh?"

Dr. Kramm nodded and Pauline sat down across from him in the booth. I took my sandwich to the end of the bar and started talking to a couple of guys from the neighborhood who were treating hangovers with Tony's assistance. I was there about five minutes and then Pauline came up and tapped me on the shoulder.

"You can go back now," she said. "Thanks."

I got down from the bar.

"Hey," she said softly, "is he a real doctor?"

"Yes," I said.

"Okay, thanks."

I went back to the booth. Dr. Kramm had finished his beer and was brooding into the empty glass.

"Another drink?" I asked him.

"No," he said. "I'll buy a bottle to take back."

Back where? I thought in sudden panic.

He read my mind.

"Look," he said. "This may sound funny as hell, childish, but—could you put me up for the night? I noticed you have that couch in your office—"

"Well—" I said.

"I know it sounds so goddam odd. But you see, I'm not altogether well. If I go home alone—and I'll be drinking and thinking about—things—and I have plenty of means handy to wipe myself out without going through any great distress—"

"I understand," I said.

"Naturally, I'll pay you for your time, the accommodations."

"We can worry about that later," I said. "You're welcome to the couch, if that will do it for you."

"It will certainly help."

"What about tomorrow night?" I asked. "And the next, and the one after that?"

"One day at a time," he said. "One night. One hour after another."

"All right," I said.

He wouldn't let me pay for anything. On our way out he bought a bottle of bourbon, and we took it over to the office. It was about five-thirty and getting dark. He had himself a couple of belts from the bottle. I declined to join him. I was trying to decide whether he would expect me to stay awake all night to make sure he didn't do himself in.

"You must know something about violence," he said suddenly.

I was startled and had no ready answer. For another thing, I didn't understand the question.

"I see it from time to time," I said. "Or the effects of it. Why?"

"I was thinking of—where it comes from."

"I don't know much about that," I said. "It stands to reason that if somebody gets pushed too far, he's going to push back. It happens all the time."

"Now you're getting to it," he said.

I wasn't sure what he expected of me. It wasn't my favorite subject. The violences I had observed were better forgotten.

"I once knew of a woman," I said, "about thirty, with a disposition so mild and sweet she was like—molded out of honey. She had three young children in a nice house in a good neighborhood. Her husband was good to her and had a good income. She had a car of her own—everything she needed. And one night she strangled her youngest child, cut the throats of the other two, and was attacking her husband with the same knife when somebody finally stopped her."

The doctor was nodding.

"She was locked in," he said.

"I don't know," I said.

"Take an obvious example. You get violence in prisons because those people are locked in. You also have a lot of seething neuroses to begin with. But part of the violence is just because they can't get out."

"I guess so," I said.

"People lock themselves in, inside themselves."

"Every man his own turnkey."

"Exactly," he said.

That seemed to be as far as he wanted to take it, and it was fine with me. We sat around till it was dark and then we walked over to Michigan Avenue and up to the corner drugstore, where he bought a toothbrush and some other things.

We turned in at about ten o'clock. He said he'd have to get up by eight in order to get home and dress and get to his office by ten. I said that if he was asleep, I'd wake him.

I had been asleep, I guess, for about half an hour, when he woke me. There was a heavy thudding sound followed by two lighter thuds, as if he had fallen out of bed and bounced. This, of course, was impossible. By the time I got out there, he was standing in the middle of the room in his shorts, and he was pounding his left palm with his right fist as if he would knock it off the end of his arm.

"Trouble?" I said, standing out of reach.

He wheeled and after a moment remembered who I was.

"Oh—" he said. "It's you. Sorry if I made a racket."

"Bad dream?" I said.

He moved his head vaguely.

"A name—" he said. "I remembered the name of a guy —somebody Lorrie knew—a bad guy—"

He had begun to shake. It was cold in the room.

"Maybe if you get back in bed and relax," I said, "it will come to you."

"Like a racketeer—"

He started toward the desk, groping.

"I need a drink," he said.

He was feeling around over the desk, searching.

"I'll turn on the light," I said. "Will you go back to bed then, after you have a belt?"

"Yes—yes—"

I snapped the switch and he found the bottle and picked it up. His hand was shaking.

"Big Danny!" he shouted suddenly.

Some of the whiskey sloshed out of the bottle and dribbled on his chin. He slammed it down on the desk and I caught it and put the cap on.

"Big Danny," he said. "He had some kind of a thing over her. She was afraid of him."

"Is that all you know? Just Big Danny?"

"That's all. She wouldn't tell me anything else about him. But he was bugging the hell out of her."

"All right," I said, waiting by the light switch. "I'll remember the name."

He was leaning on the desk with one hand, beating it rhythmically with his other fist and shaking again, as if with cold.

"Big Danny," he repeated.

I could see the violence in him now all right, like a mottled lacework under the taut skin of his face and neck.

He hadn't trusted himself to drive the day before, so in the morning I drove him to his apartment, which was out on the North Side. He was quiet, but seemed less desperate. Nothing more had been said about the assignment, and I had been thinking it over. I thought that if I should refuse to help him, he would very likely take it on himself, and it would be hard to predict what would happen. There was also the possibility that Lorrie King really had been involved with someone who could have driven her to suicide, and if the doctor should find out who, it might be necessary to restrain him or divert him.

The doctor didn't mention it till I pulled up in front of his building.

"Will you help me?" he said.

I hesitated judiciously, then nodded.

"I'll look into it," I said. "You understand, you may be mistaken. There may be nothing to find."

"All right," he said. "But you will look into it and if there is anything, you'll let me know?"

I hesitated again.

"Yes," I said finally, "I'll let you know."

"I'll give you some money," he said.

"There's no hurry about that," I said, "but I'll need a key to Miss King's apartment."

"Sure," he said. "If you'll come up, I'll give it to you, and I'll write you a check."

We went up there. He had a comfortable, unostentatious bachelor apartment, plainly furnished, except for some expensive-looking art on the walls. He took a key and a checkbook from a desk drawer and sat down.

"When did you last see Miss King?" I asked.

"Five days ago," he said.

I must have looked puzzled. "I've had a heavy night schedule this last week," he said.

There was something else. I waited for it.

"And," he said, "we had a quarrel. Not bad enough to break us up, but bad enough. It involved—a third person."

I waited while he finished the check, tore it out of the book and handed it to me. It was made out for five hundred dollars.

"All right for a start?" he said.

"Yes," I said. "I'll make an accounting."

"I don't care. Just find him. Find out who it was."

"Who was this third person," I asked, "that you quarreled about?"

"An artist named Dillon," he said. "Byron Dillon. A goddam faggot. He was a friend of Lorrie's."

"You didn't have anything to worry about from him, did you?"

"Well—he'd been giving Lorrie a bad time. I picked her up at his studio. We were going to dinner, and he

23

came tagging along; they had some kind of beef going and it was—very messy. I didn't help it any. I lost my head. Later I smoothed it over, by telephone, with Lorrie. But it was a bad night."

"Byron Dillon," I said. "Is he a good artist, or well known?"

"I guess so. He's well known, yes. Anyway, around town."

"You say he'd been fighting with Miss King?"

"Yes. In some way. I don't know the details."

"All right," I said. "Miss King left nothing in the way of a farewell note?"

"No, nothing."

"I'll get to work," I said. "I'll have to ask you to remember that there may be nothing to find."

"Yes," he said. "But dig deep."

"What was her address?"

He told me where she had lived and the apartment number.

"Okay," I said. And from the door, I asked him, "You all right now?"

After a moment he nodded.

"I think so," he said. "I think I can live now. At least—"

"You better plan on living a long time," I said. "Because this may take a long time."

"Yes," he said.

I nodded goodbye and went out. Then I turned back, knocked and got let in.

"You have a picture of her?" I asked.

"Only a portrait."

24

"Could I see it?"

"Certainly, it's in here."

The portrait was in the bedroom. It was a large picture. She was seated on a low stand, leaning on one hand, her face turned up. In the picture she was quite beautiful, with a long, slender throat, and her face was lean and clean-cut, with a firm chin. Her hair was rolled formally on her shoulders. The hand she leaned on was slender and her bearing was aristocratic, but without stiffness.

"Is it a likeness or an impression?" I asked.

"It's a good likeness. It doesn't flatter her."

"Who painted it?"

"An artist named Schramm, a good portrait man. He teaches at the Institute."

"I'd like a picture I could carry," I said. "Could we make a photograph of this?"

"I guess so."

"I'll arrange it. When will it be convenient?"

"Any time," he said. "I'll ask the manager to let you in."

"All right," I said. "I'll go now. Be careful."

He nodded, even managed a thin smile, as I left him.

3

I DROVE BACK to the neighborhood of her apartment, which was pretty much my own neighborhood, on the Near North Side, and got some breakfast. The story of Lorrie King's suicide was in the morning paper, and I read through it while I ate.

Her age was given as twenty-six. There had been no note, no goodbye. A maid had discovered her in the bathtub, had fainted, then roused herself and called the police. An autopsy disclosed that she had died of drowning, despite the evidence that she had cut her wrists and swallowed sleeping pills. There had been no other signs of violence. The apartment had been in good order and there had been no sign of visitors. Police had closed the case as a suicide.

Aside from the death itself, there was little information. Lorrie King had been active in art circles, locally and to some extent internationally. She had sponsored an exhibit of French painting at a local gallery, and she had served on committees with cultural responsibilities. She had been a member of a charitable women's organization called the Big Sisters and of the Junior League. Her mother was the prominent society figure Mrs. Corinne King, who could give no explanation for her daughter's suicide and who was in seclusion under a doctor's care. Miss King was not married, but had been engaged to marry Peter Kramm, M.D. When questioned, Dr. Kramm said he had not seen Miss King for four days and was at a loss to explain the suicide. No other persons had been questioned. Funeral services would be held on October 17—that would be the next day.

I put the paper away and finished my breakfast. It was no satisfaction and I did it because it was necessary, the way it's necessary to have a tooth filled. The portrait of Lorrie King hung before my eyes and I couldn't make it go away.

She left no note, I thought. She meant it to work, be final, complete. It will take a psychiatrist to explain it.

I left the table, got to a phone booth and called Dr. Kramm's office. He came on right away.

"Did Miss King ever have psychiatric help?" I asked him.

"I don't—" he began, then paused. Then, in a startled voice, "I don't know! How could it be I wouldn't know? She didn't tell me everything in her life, but she would have told me about that."

"Not necessarily."

"She never used any of that terminology, the way a lot of psychiatric patients do."

"I was just wondering," I said. "It might have been helpful if she had seen a doctor."

"She was no hypochondriac," he said. "I know I was the only doctor she had seen for several years, and she saw no other after she came to me."

"That you know of," I said.

"Yes," he said thoughtfully, "that I know of."

"All right," I said, and hung up.

Her apartment was Number 1016 in a new luxury building on the lake front. I could count on the probability that after twenty-four hours there would be no police lingering about and no disposition of the apartment itself. Also there would be little likelihood that my visit would be noticed. Part of the management's business would be to avoid noticing such events.

The apartment was larger and more sumptuous than the doctor's, but I could lay some of that to the difference between masculine and feminine. As far as I could judge, the furnishings and decor were tasteful and reserved. The only unusual aspect was the great number of pictures and their variety of color, subject and framing. They weren't decorator pictures, but had been selected by someone who understood what she was doing. Consequently they were a riotous jangle of color and design on three walls of the living room. The fourth wall was a window overlooking the lake.

Beyond was a den, furnished with a simplicity that contrasted with the gallery effect of the living room. A studio couch was covered by a plain gray spread. There was a small desk with a matching chair and over the desk a single picture, the portrait of a young girl with blond hair. I couldn't tell, from my memory of the portrait in the doctor's apartment, whether it was a likeness of Lorrie King.

I tried the desk drawer and it opened. In it were a couple of address books, a small sheaf of letters, a calendar pad and some plain stationery with envelopes. I laid the address books and correspondence on top of the desk, closed the drawer and went on.

There was a hall, with linen closets, leading off the living room past the den. The bedroom opened to my right. It was nearly as large as the living room and similarly sumptuous, but with fewer pictures. Those in the bedroom were abstract, in quiet tones. There were no portraits and no violent colors. The bed was queen-size, neatly made and covered with an impeccable satin spread. The room contained an antique chaise longue, but the rest of the furniture was modern. A full-length mirror in a walnut frame hung on one wall. Looking into it, I could see behind me the entrance to a spacious dressing room. Beyond that would lie the bathroom.

On a bedside table stood an easel photograph of an older woman with a severe face, but handsome, with high-piled white hair. An inscription read: "Love—Mother."

I pulled back the satin spread and found that the bed had been stripped. There was only a mattress. This wasn't too strange, and I replaced the spread and went around the bed into the dressing room.

Her wardrobe was adequate but not spectacular. A capacious closet was filled with dresses, two coats, a good many skirts and blouses—among them a number of tweeds—and a shoe rack held several pairs of formal and informal shoes. All in all, it wasn't the profusion of apparel you might expect a rich girl to have on hand.

I searched the drawers of a dressing table across from the wardrobe. They contained feminine necessities of an ordinary kind and also baubles and odds and ends of what might have been souvenirs: some plastic cocktail picks of various colors and shapes, an elegantly bound wine list from one of the city's better restaurants, a silver chain and pendant in the form of a dagger.

I had closed the last drawer, lower left, and was turning away, when I hesitated, turned back and opened it again. Mostly it was full of used stockings, in a wild tangle, unmatched and scarred by runs. But underneath the pile I had caught sight of a scrap of white paper.

I dug down to it and pulled out a white envelope, letter-size, worn and wrinkled, blank on both sides. It was thin but had palpable contents. These turned out to be some scraps of paper no bigger than matchbook covers, with legends scrawled on them in pencil or ink. Though legible, they were meaningless at a glance. One read: "St.-Rnd. 7"; another, "Edgw. 9"; another, "MF,5." Also on each was a short-form date, such as "3–21–63.'

I flipped through them hurriedly. The dates appeared to range over a period of about two years, starting that long before her suicide.

Races, I thought. She was gambling.

But then I thought, there wouldn't be any need for her to be secretive about that, nor to save all those chits from so far back.

I folded the envelope once and put it in my pocket. I checked the drawers of the dressing table again, thoroughly, and found nothing of interest. I opened a closed door and went into the bathroom.

It was immaculate, spotless, gleaming white and chrome. I looked into the scoured tub and tried to visualize the desperate, beautiful body, limp and bleeding in the deepening pink of that last bath. But all I could manage was the portrait, a stiff, angular object that wouldn't bend into shape to fit the nightmare.

It was depressing and futile there and I left the room, closing the door, and returned to the den, where I had found the address books. I sat down, switched on a lamp and started looking through them.

The first, a small, worn, leatherbound book, was indexed with alphabet tabs. Nearly every page was filled, in a somewhat cramped but neat and legible hand. It was an international assortment. There were names and addresses and telephone numbers in London, Paris, Rome, Tokyo, Hong Kong, and even Cairo and Istanbul. There were addresses of many galleries and shops. Among the individuals there were more women than men and a good many apparent couples. There were no names that I recognized, which wasn't surprising.

The other book seemed to be mainly local. It was not indexed and the entries were more careless and haphazard. But this was the one that was most important to me, and I put it in my pocket, along with the envelope from the dressing room, and replaced the other in the desk drawer. I had no reason for leaving it behind except the old axiom: If you get caught with stolen property, the less of it the better.

There had been, during my stay at the desk, a persistent odor of tobacco, stale and remote but lingering. I had seen no signs about the place that Lorrie King had been a smoker, and Dr. Kramm hadn't smoked at all. I began sniffing around, doglike. The trail led downward. There was a small wastebasket under the desk, half filled with scraps of paper and wisps of ink- and lipstick-stained tissues. I carefully lifted out a layer of scraps, most of them bills from department stores and dress shops. I made out two or three dates, three or four days previous. I pushed aside some tissues and found a cigar butt, of the type with an attached mouthpiece, yellowish-white. I laid it on one of the scraps on top of the desk and felt deeper. There were more bills, dated farther back. More tissues, a telephone message from the desk downstairs. The caller had been a Mrs. Murphy. I went all the way to the bottom and found no more cigar butts, nor any other traces of smoking, not matches, not loose tobacco.

I sat for a while, gazing at the cigar butt, reached for the telephone on the desk, thought better of it and picked up the first item in the pile of letters. Somebody knocked at the door.

I waited, looking at the cigar butt.

Lorrie had a visitor, I thought. Didn't stay long, long enough to finish smoking one cigar.

The knock was repeated.

Go away, leave me alone, I thought.

I picked up the cigar butt and the scrap of paper and laid them gently in the wastebasket, then lifted some of the recently dated scraps and spread them over the butt.

This time the knocking was followed by a masculine voice, demanding in.

Couldn't be the manager, I thought. He wouldn't expect anyone to be here, unless he had noticed me coming to this specific apartment, which was unlikely.

Couldn't be Dr. Kramm, whose office was far away. He wouldn't have had time to make it.

Couldn't be the custodian or superintendent. He wouldn't stand there knocking, he'd let himself in.

It might be—it just might be—some friend of Lorrie King's who, by some quirk, didn't know anything yet. Somebody just dropping by.

In which case it was my job to check it out.

I put the letters back in the drawer, got up and walked through the living room, unlocked the chain bolt and opened the door. A guy stood outside. About my size, younger than I but not a boy; dressed in a low-priced, somewhat baggy suit, heavy-duty reinforced shoes, and a soft hat. He was almost certainly a cop; he had the aura of a cop.

There was a cigar in his mouth, a half-smoked cigar in a yellowish mouthpiece.

4

He didn't let me linger in doubt. Without removing the cigar he took an I. D. card from his inside pocket and showed it to me. His name was Saunders, Clay Saunders. He was a sergeant of detectives; he was thirty-seven years old and the photograph on the I. D. was a good likeness. It emphasized the square fullness of his lower jaw, a feature that made him look narrower in the skull than he actually was.

"All right," I said.

He put the I. D. away.

"And who are you?" he asked.

I told him. He didn't say anything, but waited, and I took out my license and showed it to him. He nodded.

"I've heard of you," he said.

He came on into the room, puffed his cigar alight and glanced here and there.

"Lady died here yesterday," he said.

"Yes," I said.

"Lorrie King."

"That's my understanding."

He shook his head, took out the cigar, looked at it and put it back in his mouth.

"Too bad," he said. "When I got here, they hadn't taken her out of the tub yet. Beautiful girl. Break your heart to see her laying there dead."

My lead drifted down the drain with the memory of Lorrie King's blood. He had been there the day before. He smoked cigars. He had ditched one in the wastebasket. All in line of duty.

"I've seen a picture of her," I said.

He gave me his attention.

"Well," he said, "if I'm not too nosy, what are you doing here?"

I let him wait. I couldn't see that he had any authority for asking. On the other hand, he was on the cops and he could give me trouble.

"This was a rich girl," I said. "Lots of insurance."

I was far out. I knew nothing about her insurance, if any.

"Yeah," he said. "What company do you represent?"

He might know; probably not, but he might.

"She spread it around," I said. "She had a policy with Northwestern Mutual, not too big; it's not a big outfit. But it was suicide and—that's the way it goes."

He thought about it. I had made up the name, because the chances were he wouldn't check it out, and if he should check it out, he would be outraged but helpless to nail me down. Because it didn't make any great difference, and that much I knew and so did he.

"How did you get in?" he asked.

That was a nice one. He could check out whether the manager had admitted me. If I had picked my way in, he'd have a sort of case against me.

"I had a key," I said.

"Oh."

"The beneficiary of the policy had a key."

"What beneficiary?" he wanted to know.

End of the line. Resistance time.

"I'll have to have more grounds for the questions," I said, turning away.

He followed me into the den, where I sat down at the desk and he sat on the couch nearby. There was some silence.

He knocked on the door, I thought. How did he know there was someone in here? He must have been watching.

"I thought this case was closed," I said.

His jaw widened, tightened, then relaxed. He didn't like the probe.

"Sure," he said. "Clear case—suicide. But we hate to just let it go at that, for a while anyway."

"What's wrong with it?"

"We like to be sure," he said.

He was getting out on his own limb now. They didn't like to be sure at all. They had enough to do. They liked it to be closed and forgotten.

"I guess so," I said. "It would be possible for someone to push the sleeping pills down her throat, strip her, force her into the tub, cut her wrists while she was still awake and hold her head under until she drowned—and not leave any traces."

His jaw went very hard this time.

"I remember about you," he said. "You got high-placed friends in the department."

"I know some of the fellows," I said.

"You're a lucky man."

His cigar had gone out. He removed it, inspected it

briefly and sourly, then, without looking, he tossed it in a gentle arc, over my knees under the desk and into the wastebasket. A direct hit. I followed its trajectory with interest, then looked him in the face. He looked back and he knew I had noticed.

So there'll be this thing between us, I thought, and he won't be able to get it off his mind. It will gnaw at him, ratlike, and eventually he will have to do something about it.

When, I wonder? How?

"You ever hear of an artist named Byron Dillon?" I asked.

"How would I hear of an artist, unless he had a record?"

"That's what I was wondering. He's a reputed homo."

"We got a million."

"All right," I said. "Just asking."

"Ask some more," he said. "I'm interested."

I got up from the desk. Obviously he was set to outwait me, and I declined the contest.

"That's the only one I've got," I said. "So long, see you later maybe."

He followed me through the living room to the door. To the right of the door, at eye level on the wall, hung a small painting, a still life: daisies, ferns and some fruit banked around a vase. It didn't look like much to me, but I was no judge. It was colorful. And it was signed "B. Dillon."

Both Saunders and I looked at it.

"Was Byron Dillon the beneficiary of that policy?" he asked.

37

"No," I said. "I just happened to come by that name. No connection with the policy that I know of."

"What if we find she was murdered?" he said.

"Then it's double indemnity. We'd just as soon accept the first verdict."

"Juries render verdicts," he said, "not police."

"I know," I said. "Goodbye. Nice meeting you."

He let that go.

Leaving the building, I thought about the possibility that Lorrie King had been murdered. My description of it to Saunders had been only for needling. There were ways in which she might have been killed and few signs left to indicate it. But it would be an intricate, difficult thing. It would be almost impossible.

Byron Dillon had an apartment and studio near the Oak Street beach. I left my car where it was parked and walked over there, a five-minute walk.

Nearby, I thought. She could have seen a lot of him. If she liked his work, she probably dropped in from time to time. She would feel all right about it, considering his inclinations. Not that she was the kind to be over-prudent.

Thinking about what she had been like was disturbing, and I pushed my mind away from it. I was getting attached to my view of her and feeling sorry she was gone, and that was not a useful state of mind.

I had to ring Dillon's bell three times before I got a response. When somebody finally opened the door, it turned out to be a smallish figure, dressed in a Japanese yukata, plain black with a small embroidered design. I could see he was male, though it required a good look. He appeared to be sixteen or seventeen years old, but was almost certainly older.

"Mr. Dillon?" I asked.

"He's having coffee. Will you come in?"

I fought down a certain old-fashioned, irrational distaste and went in.

"Is it about Miss King?" he asked as he closed the door.

"Would it have to be?" I said.

"No, but it's likely," he said. "This way."

I followed him through a lushly furnished living room into a dinette, where Byron Dillon, likewise in a Japanese robe, but a large, less effete-looking man, was sitting at a glass-topped table over coffee and a slice of rye toast. Beyond the living room, through a partly open door, I had seen a roomy studio.

"I'm Byron Dillon," he said. "Sit down. Have some coffee?"

"Thanks," I said, sitting.

I got out my license and showed it to him. He nodded casually.

"What's on your mind?" he asked.

"Lorrie King."

His face showed pain.

"A dear friend of mine," he said. "I'm sick that she— did that to herself."

"Have any suggestions as to why she did it?"

He shook his head. He was a good-looking fellow with a forthright manner. He had no obvious suspect gestures, such as with his hands, which were large and workmanlike, an artist's hands. There was an emotional intensity when he spoke that wasn't always appropriate from a masculine viewpoint.

"I tell you the truth," he said, leaning heavily over the table, "if ever I knew a so-called healthy woman, she was it."

The "so-called" might be revealing, or it might merely be scientific.

"She had several of your pictures," I said. "Was she a good judge, a good collector?"

"A good collector," he said, "is anyone who will buy the stuff. But yes, she was a good judge. She knew a lot about it and she knew what she liked. Sometimes I think she bought pictures she didn't especially like, because she thought I needed the money. She was very generous."

"What was she like?"

He finished his coffee and his friend got up and went to the kitchen and came back with another pot. He poured from it, for Dillon and me and for himself, then went back to the kitchen. He never did show up to finish his own coffee.

"Well," Dillon said, "she would come in here—she was quite lovely to look at; dramatic but never outlandish. She had exquisite taste. She was—lonely. That's the only word I can think of. And in her loneliness, she had this kind of humility. She was always asking, asking— never telling. She wanted to know everything about the process of art. 'How do you do this, how do you do that? What feelings do you have? What do you think about when you're painting?' She was like that, always questions."

"Was she friendly? A friendly person?"

"Extremely outgoing, yes, friendly. Never on the make but always gracious and friendly. She didn't have that tight, suspicious air that many attractive women have."

I finished my own coffee.

"You said she was lonely," I said. "What do you mean?"

"It's hard to describe. She was lonely for—an equivalent relationship. That sounds kind of high-flown. I mean, she was so intelligent, so empathic—she was, you understand, rare. And truly rare people— She didn't have anybody she could communicate with."

"Maybe she had you," I said.

I hadn't meant it to be double-edged, but he didn't like it. He frowned and made a gesture of impatience.

"There was nothing between us," he said, "if you're thinking of a—romantic attachment."

"I didn't mean—"

"Strictly an artist-patron thing. Not exactly patron; she didn't support me. I sell enough. But she was my best customer and we spent quite a lot of time together."

"Was all that time, or most of it, here in your studio?"

"Oh no. I visited her too. And we went here and there, galleries, sometimes to dinner, that sort of thing. Casually."

I sat there, feeling stuck. He had been more than frank and generous with his time and comment. I hated

41

to risk losing him with a hard question, but I couldn't think of a way to avoid it.

"I heard," I said, "that you and Miss King quarreled recently, about five days ago."

He didn't like it. He scowled and his mouth worked over it and I decided I had lost him. But then he cleared a little and he said,

"I don't know where you heard it, but it's a crock."

"All right," I said. "I was misinformed."

Another fifteen seconds passed. He had finished his toast and took care to wipe his fingers with deliberation.

"There was a beef, however," he said.

"Oh?"

"Whom are you working for?"

I thought about the insurance dodge and decided against it. I didn't think this guy would go for it.

"A private person," I said. "A friend of Miss King's."

"Kramm?" he said. "That doctor?"

"I can't say."

He did some more scowling.

"You might as well get the straight story," he said. "It was five days ago. Lorrie—Miss King—was here in my studio and we were having some coffee and talking and the good doctor came to pick her up. Seems they were going out to dinner somewhere and she had told him where she would be. So in he came. First time I'd ever seen him.

"So she wanted to show him some of my stuff, and I could see he wasn't too interested, but he went along. I've been doing some abstracts, kind of experimenting, and he didn't have much to say about it, just got more and more bored. But I had picked up an illustration job for an ad agency and I had that on the easel, and the first thing I knew, he was raving over the goddam illustration.

"Supposedly, this doctor, according to Lorrie, was pretty hip. So I figured that if he really *knew*, he was raving over the illustration crap just to bug me; and if he didn't know, he was a phony and the hell with him."

He stared into his empty cup and I waited. In the kitchen there were the small sounds his friend made, cleaning up. When Dillon looked up, his eyes were frank and open.

"I'm a so-called deviate," he said.

I shrugged.

"All right," I said.

"And the good doctor has a thing about that—negative. This was plain to me after about five minutes, but there wasn't much I could do about it except to sweat it out and try to keep a civil tongue in my head. After all, he was a special friend of Lorrie's.

"Anyway," Dillon went on, "he got snottier and snottier about my work and this and that and it was disturbing Lorrie, I could see. I said to him, as I remember, that nobody could please everybody and I was sorry he didn't care for my work and I certainly didn't want to keep him from his dinner reservation.

"He didn't like that—I was practically throwing him out—and he made a remark to the effect that maybe I could show him some male nudes.

"Well, this blew it for Lorrie and she clamped down on him, said it was time to go to dinner, and then she

43

invited me to go along. Naturally, I declined politely. She insisted. The doctor didn't enter into it, just stood in the corner and sucked his thumb. And Lorrie kept insisting, and it was she who was asking and finally I said all right."

Dillon got up, took his coffee cup to the kitchen, was gone for a couple of minutes and then returned.

"We went to a place on the South Side," he said. "It was a long, dismal ride, the three of us in the front seat of the doctor's Thunderbird, Miss King trying to keep some conversation going—it was pitiful."

"Why would she set up such a situation?" I asked.

"A woman will do this sometimes. I think it's from confusion. She was trying to make something up to me, her friend, because of the way the doctor had behaved. And she couldn't tell the doctor to cut out, because he was working up to an ugly scene and no telling what he'd do. So she tried to throw everything into the pot in the hope it would cook itself out, or something like that. She didn't do it out of meanness, you can be sure. She hadn't a sadistic bone in her body."

"Okay," I said.

"Well, about halfway through dinner the doctor got started again. Same old needling crap. I took it as long as I could and then I got up and excused myself. I got the money out and dropped it in front of him and said I'd prefer to pay my own way. Then I walked out by a side door.

"I was heading around to the front of the place, to get a taxi, when the doctor came charging out after me, with Lorrie right behind him, calling to him. He grabbed me and swung me around and said he ought to smash my face in. He was very grim. And I'd had more than enough, and I told him I'd be glad to meet him anywhere he cared to specify, but not in Lorrie's presence. I reminded him that I was at least fifteen years younger than he and in good condition and said I wouldn't want to humiliate him. This made him even hotter, of course, but he wasn't all the way stupid. Besides, Miss King had her hand on his arm, calling him off, and he yielded to judgment and respect. And I left.

"And that was the beef. How it could be switched to make it look like I was fighting with Lorrie, I don't know. I've told you how it really was."

I got up.

"Thanks for telling me," I said. "Sorry to have interrupted your breakfast."

"No problem," he said.

Then, because he had been cooperative and helpful, it was necessary to alert him to some possible future unpleasantness. This was tougher than it had been to ask him the hard question.

"There is a cop named Saunders," I said, "who is digging around in Miss King's death. He may call on you."

He looked at me from somewhere dark and I had that feeling of decay in my stomach, as if I had enjoyed a good meal in a well-run place and, having finished, finger bowl and all, had announced to the proprietor that it was my duty to take him out in the alley and beat the hell out of him.

"Why me?" he said.

"He came by your name."

He thought about it.

"Well," he said, "she had my pictures here and there."

"No," I said, "he didn't get it that way. He got it from me."

The look again, not for long. He nodded slightly, pushed up to his feet, turned his back and walked out of the room. I found my way out and down to the street and stood blinking in the noonday sun. A car pulled up in a loading zone and Sergeant Saunders got out.

"Well," he said, "you're speedier than Sweeney. This is the abode of the artist Byron Dillon?"

"You'll have to do your own hunting," I said. "I'll say this much, you'll be wasting your time to talk to him. He can't help."

"I'll just take a shot at it," he said. "I like to bother these fags. They're cute."

I toyed with the thought of going in with him. Maybe I could prevent some nastiness. But then I thought I'd better leave bad enough alone. Maybe Dillon would handle it all right.

I hope so, I thought as I turned up the street toward where I had left my car. I sincerely hope so, for the sake of the memory of Lorrie King.

46

5

IHAD A QUICK LUNCH at Tony's, then went to the office and spent two hours going through her local address book. I copied out the names and addresses and phone numbers, if any, and where there was no number, I looked up the name in the phone book. Some numbers I couldn't find. There were ninety-seven names of individuals and thirteen entries that were institutional, such as "Big Sisters—Lucy Hunt, etc." Some of the addresses were in dingy areas of the city and prodded my curiosity.

I drove to the Loop, went into the Public Library, and started through the files of the *Tribune,* culling items about Lorrie King, working backward from the story of her suicide. I found a good deal about her mother and various civic enterprises, but not very much on Lorrie. Her picture appeared now and then, usually in a group and in connection with an art exhibit. Once they had given her a ten-inch picture on two columns with an announcement of her appointment as chairman of the steering committee of the Big Sisters, a philanthropic social-work organization. I found no references linking her with Dr. Kramm.

In an item dated about three years previously it was announced, without pictures, that Miss Lorrie King would become the bride of Edward Rounds, an advertising executive. There was a routine identification of Lorrie King and nothing much about Rounds.

47

I remembered the name from the address book. I checked on it and he was entered at an address on the South Side in the vicinity of the University. The ink had faded; it was an old entry. There was a telephone number, but when I checked it against the latest phone book, I found no listing for Edward Rounds.

I looked through the library's collection of advertising trade magazines and found several references to Rounds, who was evidently pretty high up in the business. The latest item placed him with a firm by the name of Carson and Brady, with offices in the Loop. I left the library at four-thirty, and the girl who answered the telephone at Carson and Brady said that Mr. Rounds was gone for the day, but would be there in the morning. I made an appointment for ten o'clock.

I called a couple of photographers and found one who would go to the doctor's apartment with me and take a couple of shots of the portrait. I promised to pick him up in ten minutes, walked to my car and got started.

The doctor hadn't arrived when we got there, around five-thirty, and we had to wait while the manager decided to let us in. He had the authority all right, but he didn't like it and he was a fussbudget, so it took some time. When we finally got admitted, I left the photographer to his own devices and took a look around.

There was little to look at. He was obviously not a type to accumulate things. His wardrobe was in good condition and there was no extravagant array. On a desk in the living room was a small stack of mail of recent date. I looked at each item and each was either a bill or some other commercial form. There were no personal letters. I tried the desk drawers, which were unlocked, and they were empty except for the shallow middle drawer, which contained more bills, all marked paid, with a date, and a couple of circular letters from the American Medical Association. Then there was a checkbook in a leather case. I flipped through the stubs. The latest was the one he had made out to me for five hundred. I reminded myself to get it out of my pocket and into the bank. The others were in payment of various bills. There was one for six hundred dollars, made to Eloise Kramm. I decided that was his ex-wife. And there was one to Byron Dillon for one thousand dollars, dated three days previously.

At that point I heard a key in the lock of the front door. I had time to get the checkbook folded away and the drawer closed by the time the doctor came in. At the same moment the photographer came from the bedroom with his bag over his shoulder and a filmpack in his hand.

Dr. Kramm wasn't surprised to see us. He asked whether we had got a good picture and if so, could he have a print. He looked tired and black around the eyes. I told the photographer I'd be right along and he went out.

"How's it going?" I asked.

Dr. Kramm shrugged.

"Luckily," he said, "I had a busy day. Not much time to think."

49

"Are you all right for the night?"

Another shrug. He opened his collar and pulled off his necktie.

"I guess so," he said. "How about dinner? You have plans?"

"No," I said.

"Any place you like."

"The Men's Grill, on Clark Street?"

"Sure," he said. "I'll shower and shave."

"I'll take the photographer downtown," I said, "and meet you at the Grill at seven."

"All right," he said.

I found the photographer waiting in the car.

"Get pretty good shots?" I asked.

"I don't know. A hard subject to light, probably be a little washed out."

"How soon can you have prints?"

"In the morning," he said.

That was the extent of our conversation and I dropped him at his studio at six forty-five, found a place to park and started a leisurely walk to the restaurant on Clark.

At State and Randolph I stopped and stood around, trying to remember something. In my pocket was the envelope I'd found in Lorrie King's dressing table, with the little chits in it.

"St.-Rnd. 7," I read. State and Randolph—seven. Seven o'clock? Likely. "Edgw. 9." Edgewater Beach Hotel, nine o'clock? "MF, 5." Marshall Field, five o'clock?

Appointments. On the street corner? Rendezvous? But if so, why would she preserve these old scribbled reminders?

I put them back in my pocket and walked on and around the corner to the Men's Grill. Dr. Kramm was waiting in the bar. He was drinking beer, I was relieved to note. I ordered a bottle for myself and we sat at the bar, not talking, because we were elbow to elbow with half a dozen others.

At about seven-thirty we got a table. It was in a secluded corner, so we could converse.

"Learn anything today?" he asked me.

"I'm not sure," I said. Then, "Oh, yes, I learned some incidental things—like, the police are still interested in the thing. Still investigating."

"I thought they'd made a decision," he said.

"It's just that they want to be sure, as they say. She wasn't just anybody; she was an important person."

"Yes," he said with feeling. "She was an important person."

We got started on the dinner and he ate in a kind of dogged silence, pushing the food into his mouth, chewing till it was gone, then loading up again. I had little appetite myself, but I wasn't going to let him shame me. And I wanted him to have a good full stomach before I went into any of the other things I had learned.

Over dessert, I popped the easy one for him.

"You were meeting Miss King here and there," I said, "in the early days, going to the Art Institute, having lunch—"

51

"That's right," he said.

"How did you work that? Would you pick her up somewhere, or would you meet her?"

"At first we would meet somewhere. A restaurant, an art gallery."

"Did you ever meet her on the corner of State and Randolph?"

He looked horrified.

"Hell no!" he said. "What makes you think—"

"I'm just asking, not surmising."

"Why are you asking?"

"In her apartment," I said, "I found these little memos."

I took them out and showed them to him.

"These are all you found?" he asked.

"That's all."

"What do they mean?"

I shrugged.

"They could mean Marshall Field, Edgewater Beach—"

"They run back two years," he said.

I waited. He shook his head and rubbed his eyes.

"I don't know," he said. "As I told you, she had other things in her life besides me. I don't know whom she'd be meeting on a street corner."

"She was in this Big Sisters organization," I said. "They work with delinquent girls, I understand. Maybe she would be meeting some girl."

"Could be. She never talked about that much. I doubt she was active in it recently. But if you found one—you did, here—as late as ten days ago—"

"But I have no idea what it really signifies," I said. "Might have been something different."

We ordered brandy and coffee, and after he'd braced himself, I said casually,

"I had a talk with Byron Dillon."

"That goddam faggot—" he murmured.

"We didn't get into that," I said. "Except that he told me frankly that he was."

"What else did he tell you?"

"Well—he told me that you and he had quite a beef going, a short time ago, in his studio and later at dinner."

"You're damn right we did. He'd been bugging the hell out of Lorrie and I'd had enough. She asked me to pick her up at the studio and I did, reluctantly, and I hated him from the start and he was mincing around the place, showing his precious work, and then Lorrie—God knows why—invited him to dinner with us. I almost blew my top. But I went along with it.

"At dinner he started giving me the needle, in that sly, dirty way he has, and I was ready to let him have it good when Lorrie broke it up."

"What kind of— You said he was bugging Lorrie. I take it before this particular evening. What did he do?"

"Figure it out," he said. "She was his best customer. She was practically his bread and butter. And he knew she was going to get married, to me, and he could antici-pate that his market would dwindle, and maybe die."

"Would it have?"

"Not necessarily, but that's how he would look at it. Anybody would, that sort of thing. It's not like food and clothing and necessities like that. It's a special, personal thing. Intimate. Marriage could well change her entire point of view."

"You gave some thought to that, did you?" I asked. "Did you think her point of view needed changing?"

"Of course not! But it might have. I wouldn't have tried to change her. But the very fact of marriage."

"You were lovers," I said. "You had the relationship already, you just hadn't formalized it. But she was still interested in Dillon's work. Would a marriage license have changed that?"

He was getting pretty hot, I could see it in the muscles around his mouth and that suffusion of color under his skin.

"I don't mean to sit here and argue," I said. "I'm just trying to understand what you're saying."

He got control of himself.

"All right," he said. "I didn't like Dillon. I didn't like the idea of him and I didn't like his work."

"What did you think you could do about it?" I asked.

He opened his mouth, closed it and shrugged.

"What I'm trying to get at," I said, "is what was he actually doing to her? You say you wanted him to leave her alone."

He gestured impatiently.

"Naturally," he said, "he wasn't doing anything sexual. But he was—*distorting* her. Fooling around with her attitudes, her perceptions."

The discourse was getting thicker and thicker and was leading nowhere. I would let it go for now. He had something against Dillon. Maybe he was justified.

"I guess that's all for now," I said.

"Did you find out about Big Danny?" he asked.

"Not yet."

He was glum now and ordered a double shot of bourbon, and I got the sick feeling that maybe he would need another night of nursing.

"It's none of my business," I said, "but if you start getting loaded up again, you'll get depressed and—"

His eyes snapped at me, his jaw tightened and he was on the thin edge again.

"Depressed!" he said. "What a word."

"I'm not a specialist in terminology. All I'm trying to say is that if you're going to need personal attention through this assignment, I'll have to hire some help. I can't do it all."

"I'm sorry," he said. "I'll be all right."

"Good. Then shall we blow this joint?"

He tried to smile, but it was feeble, far from his heart. He finished his double slug and we left the Grill and walked along Clark Street to Randolph and then east toward State.

"Drop you somewhere?" I asked.

"No thanks. I took a taxi down, I'll take one home. I'm still too shaky to drive."

"You have any friends you could ask to drop in and spend the evening?"

"Yes. Maybe I'll do that."

"You have my number. If you get the answering service and it's an emergency, they'll get in touch with me."

"Yes," he said.

He lingered. I didn't like to walk away from him, but

55

I didn't want to hang around and sink deeper into the swamp of his gloom.

"Maybe we could catch you a cab across the street there," I said.

"I think I'll walk over to the park," he said. "The Institute's open this evening. I think I'll go over there."

"Good idea," I said. "I'll be in touch with you."

"All right," he said. "Good night."

I left him, feeling uneasy and relieved both. I had parked my car on the street about two blocks from where we parted, and by the time I reached it, my thighs were tense from the strain of holding to a leisurely pace. I had wanted to run from him.

It didn't help any to find a guy leaning against my right front fender: a scraggly minim of a man, with watery, washed-out eyes under a low hat brim and nervous hands that went in and out of his jacket pockets like activated pistons. I frowned at him as I unlocked the car door and he gave me a long, sidewise glance and sidled along the car to confront me.

6

Y OU'RE THE PRIVATE eye, Mac?" he said.

His voice was thin as those tasteless Swedish wafers, rasping softly between his teeth—what he had left of them.

"Well," I said, "who are you?"

"Dingo, they call me," he said. "Dingo—that's a wild like dog."

"I know," I said. "What did you want with me?"

"I got something," he said. "You might like to see it."

"What is it?"

"Some kind of material."

"What material?"

"About that broad, that lady that knocked herself off. King? Lorrie King."

"You selling it, or giving it away?"

"Well—" he ran his hand roughly over his mouth.

"If you're selling, I'm not interested," I said.

"Okay," he said. "I'll give it to you."

He reached inside his frayed jacket and his hand came out with a small brown envelope, thin and stiff. The flap was open. He slid a photograph partway out of it, then handed me the whole package. I took the photograph out, moved away toward a street lamp and looked at it.

It was a clear, sharp, brightly lighted professional picture of a nude woman in a bathtub. Her chin had dropped forward and her face was submerged to the

57

nose. It was a black-and-white photo and the water in the tub appeared muddy. Little of her figure was visible under its murky surface. She had long, light-colored hair, the ends of which were submerged. Her eyes were closed. The back of her right wrist was visible on the water, as if floating. She was dead and no longer beautiful or vibrant. I assumed she was Lorrie King.

I pushed the paper back into the envelope and returned to the car.

"This is it?" I said.

"No," he said, "there's some more. That's only the picture."

"What more?"

He rubbed his mouth.

"Guy I know," he said, "Danny—Big Danny Corelli—you know him?"

"No," I said.

"He—well, he does this and that. He's pretty big, I mean. He can tell you about Lorrie King."

"I see," I said. "Where would I find him, if I should go looking?"

"Well—out west. I can show you the way."

I tried looking at his eyes for a while, but it was impossible to hold onto them.

"What are you, then?" I asked him. "A runner for Danny?"

"Oh no, nothing like—no. I just happen to know him."

I put the envelope in my jacket pocket and opened the car door.

"Get in," I said.

He hesitated, looking both ways along the street, then slithered into the car as if somebody was after him, as I guess somebody usually was, ever since he could remember.

He directed me westward and somewhat north. It was unpleasant riding with him. For one thing, he needed a bath. Then I had the nagging worry about Dr. Kramm wandering around alone. On top of all this, I didn't feel good heading into an unknown area on the strength of a ghoul's photograph and the nervous word of a rundown punk. But the picture was almost certainly of Lorrie King—and I had the name Big Danny from my client.

"You said Danny Corelli is in this line and that?" I said.

"Yeh," he said.

"Could you break that down a little?"

"Well—you know, guy like Danny—this and that."

"Talk to me, Dingo. We've got a long ride."

"Yeh—well, Danny's got like a store. He sells stuff. And then he sometimes accommodates people around the neighborhood—if they can't make it out to the track —like that."

"Junk man?"

"Oh no, nothing heavy like that."

"Just a small-time guy," I said. "A scrounge."

"Well—no, he's pretty big, in the territory."

He snickered.

"Joke?" I said.

"Danny's big all right—a big fat guy. I mean big!"

After a while he said,

"Funny you don't know Danny, in your business."

"Why would I know a lousy punk hood?"

"Oh no!" He sounded injured and put upon. "Danny's not a punk—hood—nothing like that. He's a businessman."

"I see," I said. "Did Danny give you that picture of the dead woman?"

"Yeh—Danny."

"And told you to give it to me?"

"Uh—yeh. Danny told me to give it to you."

"How did you know where to find me? How did you know my car?"

Silence. But it hadn't been much of a question. No great trick to learning the make, model and license number of a car, given the owner's name.

"I'll put it like this," I said. "Assuming you could identify my car, how did you know where to look for it?"

More silence.

"Come on, Dingo," I said, "talk to me."

"Well, we had a kind of a thing on you."

"A stake-out thing?"

"Not exactly like that."

"Then like what exactly?"

He spread his thin hands helplessly.

"I don't know! Danny give me the picture and told me where I'd find your car. So I went there."

That was probably true. Dingo was a small guy with a small brain and wouldn't be expected to carry much responsibility.

I let him sit for a while. We were in the West Side

now, far out; the streets, largely lined by small, run-down industries and warehouses, were dark and rough. The raw weather had settled in again and drafty winds knifed into the car at this and that crevice.

"Turn right here," Dingo said suddenly.

I had overrun the intersection and had to stop and back up to make the turn. I headed into a black cavern formed by two twelve-story warehouses, bumped across a couple of railroad sidings and came into the garish red, green, and purple light of a small business section, stretching for six or seven blocks right and left. Straight ahead, across the street into which the warehouse alley dead-ended, was a wide, brightly lighted store front with a rhythmically blinking sign in huge neon letters:

DANNY CORELLI'S BIG STORE

Big neighborhood man, I thought. What would he ever have had to do with Lorrie King? And where in hell would he get that photograph?

"Where do I put the car?" I asked Dingo.

"Round in back."

He was leaning forward now, his eyes shifting at random, excited as if glad to get back home. I wondered whether he had ever been in the Loop before tonight.

I waited for some traffic and made a left turn into the busy street. Danny's store was flanked by taverns, and beyond them were other store fronts, some closed, some open for business; I saw three pawn shops within a block.

"Danny owns the joints, too?" I asked.

"Yeh," Dingo said.

"And the hockshops?"

"Oh no—just the one of them."

At the first intersection I waited again and turned right. There was considerable pedestrian traffic on the lighted main street, but as soon as I had made the turn, it was dark and deserted. A couple of old rooming houses stood square and dismal on the left side of the street, and halfway along the block an alley opened to my right. It looked as if it would run to the rear of Danny's Big Store.

"Here?" I said.

"Yeh," Dingo said, fidgeting on the edge of the car seat. "Right here."

I turned into the alley and drove slowly past the service areas of the shops and taverns on the main street.

"How did you get downtown?" I asked. "All that way?"

"Taxi," Dingo said.

So at least he could be trusted with taxi fare, I thought. Unless they had called it for him and paid the driver before they started.

The alley broadened as we approached the area behind Danny's store. There was space for several cars, and an open slot. I drove into it, stopped and turned off the lights and the ignition. Dingo started to scramble out.

"Hold it," I said.

He sat with one leg outside, holding the door open with one hand.

"Yeh?" he said.

"You've been around here," I said, "with Danny and all?"

"Sure," he said. "All my life."

"Did you ever see Miss King here, in the store, or with Danny?"

A long pause. His hand left the car door, then returned to snatch at the handle.

"No," he said, "I never."

"Did you ever see Miss King anywhere else?"

"No. No, I never see Miss King at all."

"One more. This Danny—what do I call him? Mr. Corelli?"

The snicker again.

"Jesus no," he said. "Call him Danny. Everybody calls him Danny."

"Okay," I said, "let's go then. You first."

"Yeh—" he said, and almost fell in his haste to get out.

He led me by way of a service door into a wide corridor that smelled of garbage and urine. A couple of doors opened to my right, one marked LADIES, the other, GENTLEMEN. Farther along was a kitchen, steamy with hot grease and the vapor of coffee. Looking ahead through an archway, I could see a lunch counter, stretching from back to front of the huge emporium. It looked endlessly vast and was doing a good business. The rest of what I could see was merchandise—the cheap, superfluous merchandise of the general neighborhood store, but in unusual profusion.

Big Danny carried a complete inventory, from hardware to ladies ready-to-wear, plus furniture. In a far

63

corner was a radio and television department. Flashy display cards announced bargains: DANNY'S DISCOUNT SPECIAL—SAVE WITH DANNY—DANNY MEETS ANY PRICE IN TOWN.

From the center of the main floor a wide staircase rose to a balcony, where other departments overflowed with goods, hard and soft. A string of colored lights, looped along the balcony rail, flashed on and off, interminably winking. The shoppers couldn't be numbered in the thousands, but there was a steady flow of traffic in and out.

Moving rabbitlike, with quick darting steps among the shoppers and salespeople, Dingo led me past the base of the staircase to a roped-off section extending from the back side of the stairs to the rear wall of the building. It was carpeted in red plush. Along the back stood a row of cash registers, lined up like slot machines. On a raised platform in the center of the space was a good-sized desk, and on an outsized swiveling stool with a bucket seat sat the man I took to be Big Danny Corelli.

Dingo hadn't exaggerated. This man was large. He appeared to weigh about four hundred pounds, and he had quite a lot of height. He was in his shirt sleeves and there was a stained white neckerchief under his chin, to catch the sweat that drained from his huge, fleshy face. He was completely bald, and the creases in his face were fixed in the commercial geniality you would have to have to keep such an enterprise as the store rolling. On the desk beside him was a microphone, and as we approached the rope barricade below the desk, he pulled it into position and over a loudspeaking system that covered the place thoroughly he barked his spiel. As I was to learn, he performed it faithfully every fifteen minutes throughout the evening.

"Now folks!" he boomed. "I want to call your attention to the magnificent display of flowers in the furniture department. People talk about real flowers—artificial flowers—these flowers, just received from the Hawaiian Islands, are artificial. Everlasting!

"I'm telling you—put these beautiful specimens of floral art in your home and defy—I say *defy*—your gardening friends to distinguish the difference between them and real flowers.

"Folks—real flowers fade, wither, die. I've got nothing against real flowers. But I'll say right now and I'm proud to say: The flowers in my home—the lovely roses, carnations, gladiolas that grace my table—are artificial, and I got them right here in my own store. When people say to me, 'They're artificial,' you know what I say to them? 'If you want real flowers, Jack, you go ahead and plant some seeds—and pray for rain.'"

There was a gentle, remote patter of laughter as he switched off the mike. A cashier stood at the desk, waiting. He handed up a tab; Danny glanced at it, scrawled something on it and handed it back. He pulled the neckerchief up over his face, mopped at the sweat and settled back in his bucket seat. He caught sight of Dingo, looked at him for a long second, then at me and turned away as if I had been a fire hydrant.

"Does he want to see me or not?" I said.

Dingo jumped.

"Yeh—sure he does—he's busy—"

"Me too," I said. "Do we just go under the rope?"

I started under. Dingo grabbed at my sleeve and I pulled free.

"You can't do that—"

I got under the barricade, walked to the platform and rapped on the desk with my knuckles. Big Danny swung around in his seat, frowning, the fat face shaking. It cleared as he looked at me.

"Yes, sir?" he said. "What can I do for—"

"Mac, a private detective," I said. "Your dog boy brought me."

"Oh—Dingo—yes indeed. Just give me a minute, will you?"

"All right," I said, "by the clock on your own wall."

He nodded. The deep flesh pockets in his face jerked and wiggled.

"Be right with you," he said.

He pushed a button and a man stepped up from one of the cash registers, a lean, hungry-looking guy with leather patches on the elbows of his tweed sports jacket.

"Take over, Herman," Danny said.

Herman nodded. I looked around for Dingo, but he had disappeared.

It had taken about fifteen seconds to line Herman up. It took the rest of the minute for Big Danny to hoist himself out of the bucket seat, straighten up and step down off the platform. His paunch shook like a jellied salad and he hit the floor hard. Don't ever let anybody tell you that a fat man is light on his feet.

"This way," he said over his shoulder and opened a door in the back wall of the staircase. I followed him onto a spacious landing from which another stairway descended toward a softly lighted, denlike room, the visible parts of which were richly carpeted. Danny put one pudgy hand on a stoutly built banister and made his way down the stairs. He moved heavily but quickly. I stayed with him, step by step.

He said nothing till we were down. The room was a section of an underground apartment which I took to be extensive, though I never did see anything but the one room. It was furnished as a combination office and living room. There was a massive desk, its top clear and highly polished, with another of those king-size reinforced seats. In one corner was a well-stocked bar. There were two couches, several leather armchairs and an occasional table or stand here and there. The walls were paneled in walnut, with some hangings of a rich nature. There were no pictures.

7

Danny gestured toward the bar, waddled around the desk and let himself down on the swivel seat

"Help yourself," he said.

"No thanks."

I went to the desk, got out the envelope containing the picture, slid it out and laid it down in front of him.

"Your dog boy brought me this," I said. "Why?"

He looked at it, worked his face into a position to look glum and pursed his fat lips.

"Yes," he said, "a pity, a shame. Such a lovely woman, a real good, solid woman—"

"Where did you get the picture?" I asked.

He blinked at me.

"The picture," I said. "How did you get it?"

He spread his puffy hands.

"It came my way," he said. "Let's say I have it."

"You're sure you didn't take it?"

The eyes looked at me over their shelves of flesh.

"What a suggestion," he said.

I looked at my watch.

"Danny boy," I said, "I don't know you and I don't really want to. My time is limited. Dingo had a promise of information about Lorrie King. That's why I'm here. Talk or shut up—I don't care."

"Well now," he said, "that's different. A picture is only a picture. Let's talk about the real Lorrie King."

68

"Yes, let's."

"Well, I used to see a lot of Miss King—"

"Here in the store?"

"Here and around the neighborhood. Very charitable woman—"

"I know."

He frowned at the interruption and shook some in his big seat. But I had come a long way and it would be a long way back, and I was damned if he'd hang me up any longer than necessary.

"So you know that, too," he said. "Maybe you know about the neighborhood."

"I know about neighborhoods."

"In this neighborhood—without bragging—I can say I'm a kind of—let's say big daddy. Folks come to me with problems—all kinds of problems. In this neighborhood, it's not exactly Michigan Avenue and the North Shore. We got everything here in the way of misery and every so often the professors and the social workers come down and explain it to us. And then we just kind of go along and work out our own problems our own way."

"Okay," I said, "I've got the background. Where does Miss King fit into it?"

"Well, you probably know that she was a social worker—pretty high-toned social worker—but anyway, she would be here helping out some of our girls, younger girls, you know, who would get in trouble of one kind and another, and sometimes Miss King would come to see me about it. That's how I came to know her.

"And I'll say this, I liked her. Social workers, the run of the mill, I can leave alone. But of course, she wasn't doing it for pay, and she wasn't one to preach or hang around with the forms to fill out and all that—"

"I know how social workers operate," I said. "What did you have to tell me?"

"As I say, they come around to see Big Danny Corelli. Sometimes I can help, sometimes no. I do what I can for the neighborhood. And one day here comes Miss Lorrie King with a problem of her own—personal."

He finally had my attention. He wasn't for one second believable, but now he had to be heard out. The idea of Lorrie King consulting Big Danny on a personal problem was too fantastic to pass up.

"Go ahead," I said.

He knew he had me. He was a master of spiel.

"Yes, sir. Miss Lorrie King had a problem and she came to Danny Corelli for help."

I chewed the inside of my lip to restrain my tongue. If he had to say everything twice, it would just have to be that way.

"Lorrie King had been coming to the neighborhood about six months," he said, "trying to help these girls. In that time, naturally, she got acquainted here and there— the girls' folks, their mothers and fathers, all in the course of her, uh, work. And she had got acquainted with a young fella named Anthony Russo—Tony we called him—Tony Russo. Tony had a little sister named Teresa, and Teresa got herself in trouble with a kid named—well, a kid in the neighborhood, seventeen, eighteen years old. Tony, Teresa's brother, was about twenty then, and he found out about it. And the only thing he could think of was to kill this kid.

"Miss King found out about it at the same time, and also found out about Tony's big drive, to kill the punk that got to his sister. So she set out to talk to Tony—"

"Excuse me," I said, "when was this?"

"This was—oh—a couple years ago."

"Okay," I said.

He had begun to look at his watch—an ostentatious, diamond-studded wrist watch held in place by a gold band. He was looking at it more and more frequently.

"I don't know," he said, "if you ever saw Miss King alive, but she was a real good-looking woman. And sweet —very high class, but no airs, and very sweet-tempered. I never heard her lift her voice higher than a lady should, never. So she got hold of Tony and went to work on him. And what happened—Tony Russo fell for her."

It was a little more believable now.

"When a kid like that gets hung on a woman like that," Danny said, glancing at his watch, "he is, I'm telling you, real gone.

"Anyway, she kept him from killing the punk, but she had him on her hands—everywhere; on her back, in her hair—you know. So she comes to Big Danny for help— get this kid off me!

"Well—! I know these kids. I grew up here. Some I can handle, some I can't. Best way I know is to keep 'em busy, give 'em something to do. This Tony Russo was hanging around here and there, doing nothing. Strong kid, smart, but no trade, nothing to do."

He stopped, looked at his watch, mopped his face with the neckerchief and gazed into some private space.

"You found him something to do?" I asked.

71

"Yeah—yes, I did. I got him a job. And it worked out real good for about a year."

"And that was all it took to get him off Miss King's back—just a job?"

"Well, there was a little more to it. I had to talk to him like a real Dutch uncle, believe me. I gave him the whole lecture from A to Z. And I had Miss King there a couple of times, to kind of ease him along."

"Was she any help to you?"

"Oh yes, yes sir. In fact, she made it work. She made Tony a promise—that if he would take this job and stick with it, she would let him come and visit her once a week—they would have lunch or dinner or something, and that way everything would work out for the best, and—you know how it goes."

Yeah, I thought. I know how it goes, and not like that.

No more, I thought. I don't believe Lorrie King would do that, and if she tried to do it, if the kid was really in a rage for her, he wouldn't take it.

I got up and headed for the stairs.

"No, listen," Danny said, "I'm not finished—"

I turned at the base of the stairs.

"You're finished with me," I said. "You can tell the rest of it to whomever we've been waiting for."

"Now just a minute—"

I went on up the stairs, without hurrying, and he said nothing more to stop me.

There was no sign of Dingo as I made my way out of the store to the parking slot behind it. My car was as I had left it. There were some loiterers at the mouth of the alley and I drove past them, turned right, circled two blocks and parked on the main street, a couple of blocks up from Danny's store.

I walked back slowly toward the store and came to a telephone booth. I dialed Dr. Kramm's home telephone number and got no answer. I tried the office phone, got an answering service, which offered to reach the doctor, but I declined the offer. I checked with my own answering service, and there had been no call from the doctor, nor from anyone else. I left the booth and walked along the street to where a small man stood in the shadow of a closed drugstore.

"Listen, Dingo," I said, "leave me alone, huh?"

He looked at me with overbright little eyes.

"Doin' nothin'," he said. "Just standing here."

I brooded over him briefly.

"How would you like a job?" I asked.

"What kind of a job?"

"Guide service. Won't take long."

He shrugged and edged away from me.

"Ten dollars," I said.

"Sure," he said, coming back.

"You know the Russo family? Teresa Russo?"

"Oh sure, I know everybody around here."

"You take me to the Russo house, okay?"

"That's all?"

"Not quite. That wouldn't be worth ten dollars. You show me where it is and hang around outside while I go in, and watch and see who goes in or out."

"I don't know—"

"Ten dollars," I said.

I took out a bill and let him look at it.

"Well—" he said, "the Russo—the kid got knocked off, you know—"

"Teresa?"

"No, her brother—Tony."

"When was that?"

"Three days ago. Got in a fight, got knifed."

"I see," I said. "Maybe I can console the family."

He shrugged.

"Okay," he said.

I put the ten in my pocket, took out a five and handed it to him.

"The other five when I come out," I said.

One last shrug and he started away. I caught up with him and we passed the Big Store, made the intersection and went on along the main drag for two more blocks, past the sleazy establishments that served the neighborhood.

The business places began to mingle with cheap apartment buildings, tottering frame rooming houses. The night was cold and there were few loiterers on the street. We passed a cigar store–soda fountain and there were kids hanging around inside, mostly male. I could hear the noise, but on the street it was quiet. We were passing a high, narrow tenement building when Dingo plucked at my sleeve.

"In here," he said. "Russo."

"Which floor?" I asked.

"Don't know. They got mailboxes."

"All right, Dingo. Hang around and keep your eyes open."

In the vestibule the stained, cracked concrete floor was littered with casual refuse. There was a row of brass mailboxes on one wall and I picked out the name "Russo" on a yellowed card under Number 306. Third floor.

I climbed sagging steps through an aroma that carried me back to my childhood in another, similar neighborhood; but I had no sense of being home.

A dusty wreath hung on the door of 306. It, too, had an aroma of faded perfume, the masking scent of death. When I knocked, the door rattled loosely and the wreath slapped against it. Inside I heard a flurry of voices, Italian, a woman's rising querulously; after a moment, a man's, gruff and impatient. There were heavy steps. The door opened and a fleshy, black-haired woman looked out at me.

"Whatta ya want?" she said.

"I'd like to talk to you about Tony," I said.

Her eyes rolled, settled and went suspicious.

"You from the insurance?" she said.

"No, I'm interested in Tony—and Teresa too— because of Miss King."

"Don't know nothing—Teresa?"

Her eyes were guarded now, withdrawing.

"Miss Lorrie King," I said. "She was a friend of Teresa's, a couple of years ago."

She shook her head; her big body blocked any view into the room. From behind her the man's voice asked a

75

harsh question in Italian. She turned her head and shouted over her shoulder.

"Some guy—about Tony and Teresa!"

The man loomed behind her, tall and barrel-chested in a damp T shirt. He ran his hands back through curly, graying hair and the woman gave way to him.

"Mr. Russo?" I said.

"That's me. Whatta ya want?"

"I'd like to talk to Teresa."

"She ain't home. Whatta ya want with her?"

"I want to talk to her about Lorrie King."

"King? Don't know."

"Could you tell me where I could find Teresa?"

He looked over his shoulder, as if for guidance, but the woman had disappeared.

"She's workin'," he said.

"Well, where does she work?"

He gave me a long, hard look and shrugged.

"Whatta ya want with her?"

I wasn't getting anywhere. He had a lot on his side—a guy coming around asking to see his young daughter, with a name he didn't recognize—Lorrie King. I wondered . . .

"You remember," I said, "about two years ago— Teresa was in some trouble, and this woman, Miss King, she helped her. A nice-looking woman—you remember?"

He withdrew all the way.

"I don't remember," he said.

"Will you tell me where I can find Teresa?"

"No. Nothing. You're not a cop, police?"

"No."

"Okay, then the hell with you."

He backed inside and slammed the door shut. The wreath slapped heavily once, then in a series of light, diminishing slaps. I walked away to the stairs and started down. I had made the turn at the first landing when a broad-shouldered, heavyset man in a gray suit came up on the wrong side, his head down. I tried to duck, but not in time and he caught me hard with his shoulder. We looked at each other. It was Clay Saunders, the cop. I started on down.

"Excuse me," he said.

"Sure," I said.

Down on the street, Dingo was leaning against a trash barrel, gazing at his feet.

"See anybody you know?" I asked.

He shook his head.

"Nah," he said.

"You know a cop named Saunders—Clay Saunders?"

He fidgeted.

"I don't remember—"

"You didn't see him?"

"I don't—"

"You want the other five dollars?"

"You said—"

"Where does Teresa Russo work?"

"Teresa?"

"Where does she work?"

"Oh—at the Big Store—Danny's store."

Oh Christ, I thought.

"All right," I said, "here's the money. Have a ball."

"Yeh, thanks," he said.

He skittered off down the street and I headed for Danny's store, moving fast now, thinking about Clay Saunders. And those cigar butts. And about Lorrie King and those little chits with the dates and places on them.

8

THE STORE was in the same condition as when I had left it, no quieter, no busier. At a cosmetics counter near the front door, I asked a dark girl,

"You know Teresa Russo?"

"Teresa? Sure," she said.

"What department does she work in?"

She turned and called to another girl farther along the counter.

"Hey, what department is Teresa Russo in?"

"Birdseed," the girl said.

"Birdseed?" I said.

"The birds," she said, pointing. "Over in the corner."

I went over there and they had canaries and lovebirds in cages, hanging from the ceiling, and a small inventory of pet supplies, mostly birdseed. A lushly figured young girl with a full, red mouth stood behind a counter, trying to find something to do.

"Miss Russo?" I said.

She put her hand to her thick black hair, looked away, then back, suspiciously.

"Well," she said, "what?"

"Are you Teresa Russo?"

"What if I am?"

"I'd like to talk to you."

"What about?"

"About Miss Lorrie King."

She half closed her eyes and looked at her fingernails.

"I don't know any Lorrie King."

I gave her a couple of seconds to breathe.

"Listen, Teresa," I said, "it's important. I know your brother, Tony, has just died. I'm sorry. I know something about you and Miss King. You can help me."

After a long pause, she said, "Well, what do you want to know?"

A fat woman with an armful of packages came up and asked for birdseed. Teresa in a leisurely way made up a package, stuck it under the woman's arm and went to make change. I waited, watching the front door. Finally, Teresa came back.

"I think there's a cop coming to see you," I said.

"A cop? Why? I didn't do anything—"

"I know it. I want to talk to you before he does."

"Who are you, anyway?"

"My name is Mac. I'm working for a client. It has to do with Miss King. You remember Miss King. When you were in trouble, she helped you. She and somebody else. And she helped your brother."

"How'd you know about that?"

"I just know it. Listen, I need help—"

"Well, go ahead, what do you want?"

I decided that was the family saying: "Whatta ya want?"

"I have to be sure you remember Miss King."

"Well—all right, I remember."

"When you were in trouble, Miss King helped you, didn't she?"

"All right—yeah."

"How did she help you?"

Her lush mouth worked, she drew her lower lip between her teeth, bit down on it, and looked away from me.

"I can't tell you," she said.

I chewed my own lip.

"Do you know a cop named Clay Saunders?" I said.

Her eyes went funny. Without warning, she began to cry. Then suddenly she turned and ran off along the counter into a back room. I stood there.

A middle-aged woman clerk wandered over and said, "What's wrong with her?"

"I don't know," I said.

"What was it you wanted?"

"Birdseed," I said.

"What kind?"

"Any damn kind."

She gave me a look.

"For a sick canary," I said.

She thought about that and then she picked up a package and showed me a label.

"Like this?" she said.

"Yeah. How much?"

"Sixty-nine cents."

"Okay."

She put it in a sack and I gave her the money. Teresa Russo didn't appear. I turned from the counter and Sergeant Saunders came in the front door. I stood where I was and watched him approach, not seeing me until he reached the counter. The saleslady lifted an eyebrow at him, but he ignored her and she went away.

"You again," he said.

"Yeah," I said.

He assumed an air of casualness and leaned heavily on the counter.

"One thing I hate more than anything else," he said, "is to get bugged by a private eye."

"I see your point," I said.

"You still nosing around Lorrie King?"

"I wouldn't put it that way."

"What do you want with the Russos?"

"Funny," I said, "all the Russos ask me the same question."

"Who's your client?"

"I forget."

He was on the thin edge, and shaky. I couldn't decide how far to push him.

"What do *you* want with the Russos?" I asked.

He balled his right fist, then slowly opened it.

"Look," he said, "you wipe your nose and I'll wipe mine, all right?"

"Always all right."

I started away and turned back.

"Miss Russo went that way," I said, pointing.

He made the fist again, but he didn't do anything with it.

I walked away as far as the front door. There was plenty of cover, and I lingered, watching him. He waited for some time, looked twice toward the door, then pushed through a gate in the birdseed counter and bulled his way to the door through which Teresa had disappeared. I left the store, walked to the corner and around to the rear lot.

I made it in time to see Teresa standing against the brick wall, some distance beyond the service entrance. She stood facing the wall, her face in her folded arms. I found cover behind a parked car, and after about ten seconds, Saunders came out the service door, looked both ways and found her. As he approached, he spoke and she whirled, then backed off from him, with one hand on the wall for support. They were too far away for me to hear what they said. I could see that the girl was crying and shaking her head and that Saunders was giving her a rough time.

Saunders raised his right hand, as if to slap her, and I had to hang onto the car to keep from making for him. She broke away and tried to run, but he caught her arm and pulled her back and was at it again.

I'll have to do something if he starts beating on her, I thought. Don't let him start that.

After about three minutes, Teresa stopped shaking her head and sagged heavily against the wall, listening. Finally she nodded her head. Saunders said some more and she nodded again. Then he walked away down the alley and disappeared on the side street. The girl lingered awhile by the wall, then wiped her face with both hands and went back into the store.

By now it was nearly ten o'clock and the place would be closing. I had no idea how much pressure the girl could stand, but I wanted to learn about Saunders from her and it seemed to me this would be the best time, when the encounter was fresh in her memory.

Two kitchen workers came into the alley dragging trash cans, dumping them into other cans outside the door. The glow of lights around the building went dim and I knew they were closing the place.

I walked to the side street and down to the corner, crossing to the far side, where Teresa Russo would cross if she should be going straight home. Pedestrian traffic had dwindled and few people passed. Looking down toward the store, I could see the employees leaving by the front door, in pairs, alone, three or four at a time. There was enough light to see everyone clearly, and I moved to a spot from which I couldn't miss Teresa.

I waited twenty minutes. All the front lights were out now and no more people emerged. If I had missed Teresa, it would have been in the half minute or so it had taken me to get from the alley to the corner. That was unlikely. She might have come out the back way, but then I'd have seen her en route. She might go home by a roundabout route, by the side streets, but she was a neighborhood girl and would know better than that. She would stick to the well-lighted thoroughfare.

I went to the front door and it was locked. There were some night lights burning inside, but no people in sight. There was some light showing toward the rear, where Big Danny's platform stood behind the stairs.

I walked around the corner to the alley once more and the service door stood open. A kitchen helper dragged out one more can of trash and dumped it. I started in past him and he said,

"Closed up, buddy."

"Yeah," I said. "I want to see Big Danny."

"I don't know—"

"I've got an appointment," I said and went on. He didn't say any more.

Big Danny's platform and reinforced seat were dark. Light glowed dimly on the stairway leading down to the apartment. I could hear voices, but because of some acoustical condition, they were muffled and I couldn't make out any words. I started down, hugging the wall, knowing I could be seen before I would see. The voices grew louder and more distinct. One was Big Danny's, the other was the girl's. As usual, Big Danny was doing the talking.

" . . . So I tell you straight from the heart, kid, Sergeant Saunders is the only friend you've got in the world. You go along with him or we got trouble."

She mumbled something.

"What?" he said.

"All right, I said!"

"I'm glad to hear it."

"Can I go now?"

"Yeah, you can go. But if I hear any more from the sergeant about—noncooperation, you don't have to come back."

"I don't know what he wants me to do!"

"He'll let you know. You just relax and go along."

She said nothing more. I squatted low on the step and saw her, from the knees down, approaching. I straightened, turned, and looked up at Sergeant Saunders. He was three steps above me, descending.

"This is it," he said between his teeth.

I started to one side to get around him, and he came

out with his right foot suddenly, planted it in my chest and pushed. I went backward, twisting, to get the arch in my back out rather than in. I fell heavily and rolled to the bottom of the steps. Luckily they were thickly carpeted. I was shaken, but conscious. There was a painful strain in my left shoulder. I got on my feet in a crouch and Saunders was all the way down the steps, with his pistol in his hand.

"Store's closed, Danny," he said.

"Yes, Sergeant."

Saunders brought his badge out of his pocket, mockingly, and displayed it.

"All right," he said to me, "get over there."

I backed off, straightening with difficulty. The girl was standing in the middle of the room, uncertain which way to go. Big Danny was seated behind the desk. Saunders, covering me with the pistol, made a gesture with his thumb, and Teresa Russo, without looking back, moved to the stairs, climbed up and out of sight.

That photo of Lorrie King dead in the bathtub, I was thinking. That was a police photo. Big Danny could only have got hold of it from a police source.

9

Saunders waggled his hand at me and I went to the desk. He backed off enough to stay out of reach.

"Empty your pockets," he said.

"Hold on," I said. "What have you got here?"

"I got a badge," he said. "The store is closed. Did he knock?"

"No, sir," Big Danny said.

"Ring any bells?"

"No."

"Just walked in?"

"Right."

"Empty your pockets," Saunders said to me. "I'll be glad to do it for you, but I'll make you sick first."

I believed him. I took my wallet out and dropped it on the desk. There were some scraps of paper in my pocket along with the wallet, and one of them came out and fluttered to the floor. I bent to retrieve it and Saunders put his foot on it.

"Everything," he said.

The little slips I had taken from Lorrie King's desk were in my office. But on one of those still in my pocket was Dr. Kramm's name, address and telephone number. I couldn't tell with my fingers which was which. I left a couple but pulled some of them out and tried to read them in passing. Saunders clubbed my elbow with the barrel of his pistol and my fingers went numb. I dropped the stuff on the desk.

"All right, all the pockets," he said. "Everything."

I went through them, brought out car keys, house key, handkerchief, penknife, and dropped them on the desk. Big Danny sat and watched. His pudgy hands were curled together on the desk top. He didn't reach for anything.

Saunders started pawing through my things.

"You want to prefer any charges against this man?" he asked.

"Well now," Big Danny said, "what do you think, Sergeant?"

He's asking for a cue, I thought.

"It's up to you," Saunders said. "It's your store. Did he get away with anything?"

"Don't think so. Just came down here—"

"Was your door locked?"

"Front door," Danny said. "Service door—? I don't know for sure."

"It was wide open," I said.

"Shut up," Saunders said. "What do you say, Danny?"

"I guess not," Big Danny said. "No loss."

Saunders had his out now. He had all he wanted.

"Pick up the junk," he said.

I gathered up the things and put them back where they had come from.

"That all?" I said.

"Get the hell out," Saunders said.

"Good night," I said.

I went to the stairs and up. I was still stiff, but not

88

really hurting. I was also sick to my stomach and I had a beef to settle with the sergeant.

The service corridor was dark now and there was no light or sound from the kitchen. The heavy door was closed and I pushed through it and looked at the two cars still in the rear lot. One was a big cream-colored Cadillac, which had always been there, and I took it to be Danny's. The other was a low-priced sedan, not a police car. Saunders apparently was off duty. I checked the visible registration and it was Saunders' car all right. I tried the door on the driver's side and it was locked. I walked around and it was locked on that side too. I thought about it for a few seconds, then moved close to the building and squatted behind the trash cans beside the door.

I waited about five minutes. I could tell by the heavy, flat-footed tread inside when Saunders reached the service door. I waited till he had got through it and let it swing shut, and when he headed across the alley toward his car, I hit him from behind with my right shoulder, with both arms around him, turned him and ran him into the wall of the building. He was strong and heavy and was able to drag his gun from the holster, but he hit hard enough to sag. He tried to turn on me, snaking the pistol up from his waist, and I pushed at the back of his head and banged the wall with it once more. He stiffened, then went limp. I eased him down on the concrete, got hold of his gun and tapped him on the side of the head. He went to sleep and I could be fairly certain he hadn't seen me.

Working quickly, I started through his pockets, beginning with his pants where it was tight and difficult. He had some change and a few bills crumpled in one. In one was a handkerchief. In the second pants pocket I found the key to a safe-deposit box. I lit a match to see by and wrote down the number of the box and the name of the bank, then put the key back in his pocket.

In his left jacket pocket was his badge. Some scraps of paper were there, an empty match folder, a small pocket knife. In the other outside pocket was a wadded piece of brown paper. I opened it and smoothed it out and read Dr. Kramm's name, address and telephone number. Sick again in the stomach, I pushed it into my own pocket.

His right inside jacket pocket was closed by a zipper. It stuck when I pulled on it and he stirred and made some sound. I picked up the gun and tapped him again and he subsided. I got the zipper open and found two bank passbooks, one for a savings account and the other an ordinary commercial account book. At a glance I saw that he showed savings deposits in four figures. The checking account was average, such as a cop might be expected to carry. I noted the names and locations of the banks. He was using three different banks.

I put the passbooks back in his pocket and zipped it shut. In the last pocket he had a wallet containing some money, about forty dollars, and some credit cards, an I. D. insurance card and some odds and ends of no interest. I put that back, checked through him again to make sure I hadn't missed anything. I took the car keys, went to the car, opened it and checked through the glove compartment. There was nothing except what anyone would carry—some maps, gasoline credit cards, auto club. I closed and locked the compartment, took the car keys back and put them in his pocket. Then I rolled him close against the wall, where he wouldn't be run over, and left him. I got to the side street and back to the main drag and down to my own car. The street was deserted now except for a few taverns. I drove out of the neighborhood and found a streetside phone booth. I went in there and dialed Dr. Kramm's number at home. I waited through a dozen rings and when he came on, his voice was thick with sleep.

"It's Mac," I said. "I'm afraid I'm no longer able to help you."

"What—? Say that again."

"I said I can't help you any more. I'm sending you some things—"

"Hey—wait!" he said. "What happened? You can't do this—"

"Your identity has been disclosed," I said. "Through my carelessness. It makes everything almost impossible."

"Why? I don't get it. What difference—"

"I'll explain it in a letter."

"Please, Mac—don't—let's talk it over—"

"Not tonight. Get some sleep. I'll send this material and I'll call you."

"Be sure and call me. Early in the morning."

"All right. Listen, does the name Teresa Russo mean anything to you?"

"Teresa Russo? No—nothing."

"Good-looking young Italian girl, about eighteen years old. Did you ever hear Miss King speak of her?"

"No. Well, she might have, but I don't remember."

"All right. I'll call you in the morning."

I hung up. I stood there in the booth for a couple of minutes, then left it and got back in the car. I drove down the street, parked in front of the old apartment building where I had talked to the Russo parents and climbed up to the third floor. There was no light showing under the door, and inside it was quiet. Only the wreath slapped lightly once or twice against the door in a small breeze.

I walked away from it and downstairs to the car. It took me about forty-five minutes to get home. There were no calls on file at my answering service.

I got undressed, took a long bath and went to bed. After a while I got up, found the death photo of Lorrie King and studied it. I could see now, in the bright light of the lamp, that besides the one floating hand, her kneecaps were visible just above the surface of the water, as if she had slid down, thus immersing her mouth and nose.

I turned off the light and lay in the dark with the faint sickness you have when you've fluffed on a client.

10

My telephone started ringing at seven in the morning. I let it ring for a while, then picked it up and it was the doctor.

"Straighten me out, will you?" he said. "What happened and what does it mean? Did you find out something about Lorrie?"

"Not exactly," I said. "I told you there's a cop interested in the case. I think he's more interested than he ought to be. His name is Clay Saunders. He surprised me last night and found out your name. That's what happened."

"I don't see what difference it makes. What could he have to do with me?"

"I'm not sure. I'm just trying to avoid embarrassment for you."

"Listen—please don't run out on me—"

"It's only a question of whether I can be useful," I said.

"What else have you found?"

"Not much. Are you going to the funeral today?"

"Yes."

"I have a couple of questions—let me ask you again about the Russo girl."

"I have no idea. I can look her up in the office. Maybe she came in once—"

"You might look it up."

93

"All right."

"And for another thing, how tall was Lorrie King?"

"Tall? About—just above my shoulder. I'd say five feet six. Average height."

"Weight?"

"Well—average. She had a good figure and never seemed to worry about weight. I'd guess about one-ten, maybe a little lighter. She was slender."

"Okay. Once more—you'll probably be hearing from this cop, Saunders. I advise you to go along with him and hang onto your temper, no matter what he asks you."

"All right. Sure."

"And if you hear from him, let me know right away. In advance if possible."

"Certainly. Anything else?"

"Unless you can find something on the Russo girl."

"I'll look her up."

"Then I'll be in touch with you."

"Right, thanks."

He hung up. I got up and made some coffee, read the morning paper, took a shower and dressed. I called the photographer who had taken the pictures of Lorrie's portrait and he had prints ready for me. I drove downtown to get them and had breakfast on Michigan Avenue. From there I went over to LaSalle Street and in an ancient, mistreated office conferred with a man named Howard Mulligan, C.P.A. He was nearly as old as the office and mistreated in much the same way, but he had a mind like a power-driven corkscrew and he was a specialist in financial investigation.

I gave him the information I had gleaned from Sergeant Saunders' pockets and he studied it at length without comment.

"That all you got?" he asked.

"No," I said. "One other thing—Lorrie King. I want to know about the activity to and from her accounts in the last couple of years."

"The girl that killed herself the other day?"

I nodded. His grizzled face creased in a kind of desperation.

"She's dead—I don't think so. Everything sealed up tighter than a new coffin."

"It's urgent."

"I don't know—"

"Can you try?"

"Yeah, I can try. You in a hurry?"

He held up a gray, delicate hand.

"Don't answer that," he said. "Call me tonight."

"Thanks," I said.

He shrugged and looked hopeless and I left him.

Outside I looked at the pictures of Lorrie King's portrait, and then for a while again at the photo of her dead in the bathtub. Pretty soon I put them away in the glove compartment, drove to another parking lot and put in a call to a woman named Clarissa Smith, also a specialist, but in a different line of investigation.

"You have time for a short job?"

"What job?" she said.

"Experiment—a fitting."

"What do I have to fit?"

"A bathtub."

"You all right?" she said.

95

"I'm fine. How tall are you?"

"Five feet five and one-half inches in my—uh—stockings."

"Weight?"

"It varies. Right now about one-ten."

"That's good."

"It'll do for now. What do you want of me?"

"Very simple, just in and out of the tub."

"Pictures?"

"No pictures."

"Any bystanders?"

"Only me."

"Ooh—you—aren't you getting a little mature for that sort of thing?"

"Will you do it?"

"How much?"

"Fifty."

"Plus travel time?"

"Right."

"Okay. Where and when?"

I told her seven-thirty that evening and gave her the address of Lorrie King's building. Then I hung up, killed fifteen minutes over a cup of coffee and walked to the offices of Carson and Brady, Advertising.

Edward Rounds was in his early thirties and had the fixed graciousness of a smooth salesman. He had prematurely gray hair at his temples and a crew cut, which gave him an appearance of boyishness. But he had worked his way to a high level in a big ad agency, and in order to do this, he would have had to know something about the way the world works. When I said I wanted to

96

talk about Lorrie King, his affableness was strained, but he didn't try to put me off.

"Sure," he said. "I was shocked to read about her—suicide. How did you know I ever knew her?"

"I looked it up in the newspapers," I said.

"Oh? That was a long time ago."

"Three years," I said.

He shrugged.

"Well," he said, "what do you want? I mean, what are you going to do with it?"

I got out my license and showed it to him.

"Private detective?" he said, grinning. "No kidding? I thought you guys were something somebody made up."

"I don't know," I said. "I feel real."

"Who are you working for?"

"I'd rather not say."

He got out a cigarette, frowned as the tip glowed in his lighter flame, then shrugged again.

"If I can help you—" he said.

"You were going to marry Lorrie King."

"I thought so, once," he said.

"What happened? What went wrong?"

"I don't know exactly. We just kind of—broke up. Lorrie was a peculiar girl."

"Tell me about her."

"I don't know—where to begin. What do you want to know?"

"I'm not sure. I'd like to find out what kind of woman she was."

"That's hard to say. She was, for one thing, spoiled."

"Oh?"

97

"She had all that money, you know, and she didn't have normal reactions to anything. She was a kind of a nut."

"About everything?"

"Well, no—I don't mean she was crazy. She—well, for instance, one night, we had this date with another couple and we weren't exactly smashed, but everybody was feeling good enough, and we wound up in one of those arty spots out in Old Town, near Chicago Avenue, you know?

"So it turned out that Lorrie knew practically everybody in the place, including a bunch of fags—she knew them better than anyone else. So from the joint we went to a studio. Art? Man, it was wild—if it was art. I don't know. We've got two art directors in the agency who can draw better.

"Then things began to get far out and the fags were smashed and Lorrie and the other guy's date got the spirit and he and I decided it was time to cut out, but the girls wouldn't leave. I got Lorrie in a corner and tried to talk sense to her, but she told me not to be stuffy. She was having a good time.

"The next thing I knew, the girls were taking their clothes off and a couple of the so-called artists were starting to make sketches—I don't know what anybody was trying to prove. Especially Lorrie. The other girl wouldn't have done it if Lorrie hadn't put her up to it.

"It was one of those crawly situations, with the fags and everything, and it made me sick. I finally told Lorrie that either we would leave, right now, or I'd leave without her. So she got dressed and came along. Then on the way home, she apologized and cried and got sick, from drinking too much, and altogether it was a hell of a bad night."

"Were you engaged at this time?"

"Yeah," he said. "Yes, we were."

"But that wasn't what broke you up?"

"It helped. I had a serious talk with Lorrie a couple of days later and she seemed to take it all right. She didn't give me any argument. 'I'm sorry if I embarrassed you,' she said. But then it got so we were getting into little arguments all the time, and anything I wanted to do, she would go along all right, but she wouldn't really get with it, and I never could tell whether she was enjoying herself or not, and then she started dragging me around to art galleries and places and one thing after another— we just broke up."

"Was it formal? Did you come to some agreement? Or did you just stop calling her?"

"Oh, I wouldn't do that. I told her frankly, I had doubts that we had very much in common, and she agreed with me and—it was friendly enough. No tears."

"Were there other—escapades?" I asked. "Like the one at the studio?"

"No—I wouldn't put up with it and Lorrie knew it. She never tried to get me together with those people again."

"You're married now?" I asked him.

He frowned and looked away.

"I don't see what that has to do with it."

I wondered where I had scratched him.

"Never mind," I said.

"No reason I shouldn't be, is there?" he said.

"Certainly not."

"I married a friend of Lorrie's. There was a group of them, mixed up in this charitable thing—the Big Sisters."

"I've heard of it. Was your wife active in it?"

"Yeah, for a while. But it took too much time. We've got two children now and she's busy at home."

"What sort of work did the group do?"

"I don't know much about it. Bunch of the girls, you know. In a good cause. They worked pretty hard, I guess. Had some kind of a program for unwed mothers —stuff like that."

"Were your wife and Lorrie King on friendly terms?"

He opened his mouth, closed it, looked at the top of his desk and then at me.

"Look," he said, "I've been talking freely here. How about you leveling with me?"

"I don't know what you mean," I said.

"Who are you working for? What's behind the questions? I read in the papers, Lorrie killed herself. It's official. The case is closed, isn't it?"

His hands were restless. One of them was shaking slightly and he folded them together on the desk, as if to conceal it.

"I thought so," I said. "I can tell you this much. A friend of Lorrie's asked me to run down a few things. I tried to talk the friend out of it, on this same basis, that the case is closed. But I ran into a cop, an official cop, who was still poking around in it and so I'm not so sure now."

"You mean there's a chance she was—?"

I shrugged.

"Who is this friend you talk about? Is it by any chance my wife?"

"I can't talk about that," I said, getting up. "I won't bother you any more."

At the door I turned to look back and he was sitting in the same position, his hands folded on the desk.

"Just one more thing," I said. "When was the last time you saw Lorrie King?"

His eyes did something jerky. He opened and refolded his hands, then reached for his cigarettes.

"I'm afraid I'm busy," he said.

"Okay," I said, and went out quickly.

His office was on the tenth floor. There was a coffee shop on the mezzanine and I left the elevator there and went in and ordered coffee. Along the wall beside the entrance to the coffee shop there was a row of telephones. I had nearly finished the first cup of coffee when Rounds came in, moving fast, went to one of the phones and dialed. I had no way to move in close enough to find what number he was calling or to hear what he said. He waited through what would have been about eight rings and somebody answered. He was talking and listening altogether for nearly three minutes. Then he hung up roughly and walked out, not looking around. I made a note of the time, drank another cup of coffee and left the building. My car was parked four blocks away and by the time I reached it, it was time to head for Lorrie King's funeral.

I I

It was a civil ceremony in a funeral chapel on the South Side. It was neither public nor closed. Byron Dillon was there, without his friend. Dr. Kramm was there. I was there, and so was Sergeant Saunders. The sergeant had a couple of bruises on his face, but otherwise he looked healthy enough. We examined each other at some length, but I couldn't tell whether he laid the mugging attack to me or not.

There were many flowers. Lorrie King's mother, in a thick black veil, sat up front with several others whom I took to be members of the family. Dillon and Dr. Kramm sat farther back, at opposite ends of a long row of seats. The sergeant was behind the doctor. I got there at the last minute and sat in the back row.

It didn't take long. An organ played some slow music. A man in a black suit said a few words of comfort and commended the soul of Lorrie King to heaven and the organ played again and that was all. Everybody sat still and waited while Lorrie's mother and family rose and left the chapel. And I sat and waited while Dr. Kramm went out, then Saunders and finally Dillon.

Outside in the October sunshine, some men in black loaded Lorrie's coffin into a gray hearse and Lorrie's mother and several others got into three limousines, and the cortege, escorted by two motorcycle cops, moved off in the direction of Jackson Park. The burial, I had heard, would be in a North Side cemetery.

There remained Dr. Kramm, Dillon, Saunders and I, and a few bystanders, who drifted away. Dr. Kramm was standing at the curb just outside the door of the chapel, watching the departing hearse. Saunders stood some distance away down the street. Dillon walked slowly toward the opposite corner.

When the hearse had disappeared, Dr. Kramm turned, looking for me. Saunders was standing around, waiting for something. I shook my head slightly at the doctor and he looked at something else, then walked off toward the parking lot behind the chapel. Saunders appeared to pay no attention, but he wouldn't go away.

Dillon was standing uncertainly on the corner, looking around vaguely. I waved at the sergeant, who ignored it, and strolled toward where my own car was parked on a side street. Dillon had crossed the street and was getting into a dusty Jaguar. I was in my car and started by the time he pulled away.

It was easy enough to keep the Jaguar in sight. He drove south to 67th Street and turned west. I was three blocks back when he pulled over, left the car and went into a tavern. I waited about fifteen minutes and he came out and drove two blocks, stopped again and walked away down the street. I got out and went after him. He moved in a halting, desultory way, as if unable to decide whether to go ahead or turn back. Eventually he entered another saloon and was in there nearly half an hour. When he came out, he was unsteady and he leaned against the building for some time, his head up and back, before moving on. He appeared to have left the Jaguar far behind on purpose, or to have lost track of it.

I closed somewhat behind him and the next time he turned into a drinking spot, I went in after him. He ordered a double rye and water and drank it doggedly, sip by sip, while I nursed a slug of bourbon and waited. He looked at me blankly half a dozen times and looked away. Then he began to look at me with more interest. I sat still, minding my own drink, and after a while he leaned along the bar toward me and said,

"I'm sorry—I think I know you—but I can't place—"

"You're Byron Dillon, the artist," I said.

That was all it took. Either he was gratified to be recognized, or incapable of sticking with a thought. He nodded vacantly, started to speak, thought better of it, or forgot what it had been, and returned to his drink. I sipped slowly at my bourbon.

Suddenly he twisted on the stool, looked hard at me, slid his feet to the floor and started out past me. I waited till he was clear of me and got down. He held up both hands, pushing at the air.

"Get away—leave me alone—you're that goddam—cop!" he said.

I stayed where I was, leaning against the stool, and let him back away and outside. Then I followed him to the street. He had started back toward his car and it was pretty clear he had no memory of where he had left it. He walked a couple of blocks, pausing now and then to survey the cars parked along the curb. Finally he turned into a telephone booth. He dialed, waited, hung up, evidently without an answer. When he left the booth I was nearby, waiting, and he saw me, turned quickly and walked away. I stayed a few paces behind him. We walked past the Jaguar at a pretty good clip and about half a block beyond. Then I called to him.

"Your car is back there, I think."

He wheeled, made those pushing gestures and tried to sidle past me to get to his car. He stumbled and nearly fell and I caught him and helped him back on his feet.

"Let go," he said hoarsely. "You set that lousy cop on me—you son of a bitch—"

"I'm sorry if he gave you a bad time," I said. "He's a bad guy."

"Bad guy—" he said. "He's a bad guy—you're a good guy? Good guy—bad guy—"

"Come on," I said, "I'll help you to your car."

He wrested himself from me violently and started to run toward the Jaguar. He careened into a lamp post, staggered, caught himself and managed to make it to the car door. But he couldn't get the key in the lock. I let him work on it for a while, then went up, took the key from him and opened the door.

"If you try to drive," I said, "you'll kill somebody."

"The hell with it," he said. "Leave me for Christ's sake alone!"

He dived into the car and sprawled on the seat, banging his head against the steering wheel. Then he gave up, rolled onto his face with his head in his arms and began to cry, rackingly, his shoulders jerking.

After a while I said, "All right, you went to a funeral—

105

someone you were fond of. But you can't bring her back. Tell me something—whom are you really sore at?"

No answer. I waited a long time.

"Are you sore at Dr. Kramm?" I asked.

He started up on the seat, his face twisted with fury. "The goddam good doctor—"

"Listen," I said, "the doctor gave you some money. A thousand dollars."

He leaned his head against the wheel and banged his fist rhythmically on the dashboard.

"What was it for?" I said. "What was the money for?"

"Oh the son of a bitch," he moaned. "The dirty, lousy son of a bitch—"

"Okay," I said.

"I wouldn't take his goddam money—"

"You tore up the check?"

"Yes—I—tore up—the—goddam check!"

"What was it for?"

He was extremely upset and it was brutal to keep him at it, but at the same time, he was more likely to tell me something then than he might be when under full control. I waited, leaning against the open door of the car. He put his face against the back of the seat and his strong artist's hands worked at it.

"Oh Lorrie—Lorrie—!" he said.

Something sparked him then and he looked at me with a kind of recognition.

"The bastard—" he said. "I had this picture—a good picture, one of the best I ever did. I gave it to Lorrie—wedding present—"

He buried his face again and his shoulders throbbed.

After a while he moved his face enough to talk and he said,

"And the goddam doctor—you know what the son of a bitch did—he sent me a check for a thousand dollars and he said he couldn't accept a wedding present like that from me."

My stomach contracted.

"He couldn't accept—a wedding present—"

I looked at him, squirming in his pain on the seat of the car, and I said,

"Stay there. I'll call somebody to take you home."

He didn't say anything. I still had his car keys and I took them with me back to the phone booth. I looked up Byron Dillon in the directory and dialed. There was no answer and I stood near the booth, waiting, keeping my eye on the Jaguar. I didn't think he would go unnoticed for long with the door open and his legs hanging out like that, so I walked back and tried to get him all the way inside so I could close the door. But he lashed out at me with his feet and I gave it up. I went back to the booth and dialed again and a voice answered. It was a light, clear voice, tense and guarded.

"Byron—?" it said.

"No," I said. "Byron is here, on the street, in his car—"

"He went to Lorrie King's funeral."

"Yes. And then he hit a few bars and he's—"

"Oh God!"

"So I was wondering if you could get over here and drive him home. He won't let me help him."

I told him where we were.

"It will take a while. I'll have to get downtown and take the I.C. and then a bus—"

"Take a taxi."

"A taxi! My God, it would cost—"

"About five dollars. I'll pay for it."

"Oh no—"

"The reason to hurry is that he's in bad shape and if the cops find him lying in the car, you know how it goes."

"All right. I'll be there as soon as I can."

"Thanks."

I hung up and went back to the Jaguar. Dillon had quieted down some. He kicked feebly when I touched his shoes, but was not really fighting, and I managed to fold him onto the seat and get the door closed. Then I backed into the shade of a store front and waited for his friend to arrive and take care of him.

It was about twenty-five minutes before he got there, in a taxi. I went to help pay for it, but he wouldn't let me. He was a very nice-looking young guy, more mature now in street clothes, and intelligent, and very concerned about Dillon. He went straight to the Jaguar and looked in.

"Byron—?"

Dillon moved sluggishly on the seat and it was some time before he recognized anyone.

"Frankie—" he said then. "Baby—"

"Come on," Frankie said. "I'll take you home."

"Yeah—home—"

"You'll have to straighten up. I mean, so I can get in."

I reached to give Dillon a hand, but he pushed me away. Frankie helped him sit up and he stayed up pretty well, though his head lolled helplessly. Frankie went around and got under the wheel and got it started. He leaned across the seat to say,

"Thanks. He might have got killed."

I nodded and backed off and they drove away.

It was long after lunchtime now and I found a coffee shop and had a ham sandwich and some coffee. When I finished, I put in a call to Mulligan, the accountant. He wasn't in and nobody at the answering service could tell me anything. I called my own answering service and there had been no calls. I decided against calling Dr. Kramm during office hours, found my car and drove to my office.

Dingo, the dog boy, was waiting for me just inside the vestibule. I pondered briefly over the way he always seemed to anticipate where I would turn up.

12

"Hello, Dingo," I said.

"Yeh—hi."

"What've you got?"

"Oh nothin'—I was just—"

"Passing by."

"Yeh."

"How's Big Danny?"

He shrugged. I leaned against the door and waited. You ask these characters questions, it only confuses them.

"—Russo—" he said finally.

"What about it?"

"Teresa."

"All right. Teresa what?"

"You wanna see her?"

"I don't know. Should I?"

He shrugged some more. It was like an all-over twitch, as if somebody were tickling the soles of his feet.

"Does she want to see me?" I asked.

"Yeh."

"Is she working tonight?"

"Nah."

"Can she get over here?"

Another shrug.

"All right," I said. "Nine-thirty tonight. You put her

110

in a taxi. I'll pay for it when she gets here. And I'll send her back."

"Okay."

I waited.

"Is that all?" I asked.

"Yeh, I guess so."

"All right. Goodbye, Dingo."

He lingered, either reluctant to leave my company or waiting for a handout. I didn't come up with the handout and after a minute or so he turned with that vague, shrugging twitch and went down the steps. I waited till he was half a block away toward Michigan, then went inside.

I looked through my mail, which was nothing to get excited about, undressed and took a shower and lay down for a rest. I would have fallen asleep, but the telephone rang at twenty minutes to six. The voice, a man's, was strange to me. It was quick, breathy and businesslike.

"You have a few minutes?" it said.

"For what?"

"Talk."

"Talk about what?"

"Lorrie King."

"I don't know who you are."

"Sharkey. Andrew Sharkey."

"Well, Mr. Sharkey, I have an appointment—"

"Won't take long. I'm right around the corner. Come right over. Think I may have something you'd be interested in."

The way he said it gave me pause.

111

"You're an eye? A bird dog?" I said.

"Right."

"All right, come on over. I've got about fifteen minutes."

"Plenty of time," he said, and hung up.

I was dressed when he arrived. He was a stocky, young-ish guy with a pock-marked face, otherwise undistinguished. He had a jovial front, except for his eyes, which were restless and inquisitive. This, I thought, would make his professional life difficult, if he really was in the business.

I gave him a chair and sat down at my desk. He had a mannerism with his mouth that made it seem as if his tongue and lips formed the words too soon; you didn't hear anything till after he had spoken.

"You said something about Lorrie King," I said.

"Yeah."

A pause.

How much will it cost? I was thinking.

"I'm not interested in every detail of Lorrie King's life," I said, "or, for that matter, her death."

"Well, yeah, I dig you all right. But I figure you'll be interested in this."

"You have a client?"

"Oh, you might say. But no direct connection. Just glancing off, you know?"

He was too damn cryptic.

"This information," I said. "You're selling it? For cash?"

A look of pain twisted his face.

"You got it wrong," he said. "I'm not peddling. Just trying to help out a fellow worker."

"Okay," I said. "What have you got?"

"Just one thing—" he said.

Yeah, I thought. Sure. No cash. Just one thing. Always just one thing.

"All right," I said, "let me have it."

"This is confidential, just between us."

I stared at him.

"What can I say?" I said. "How do I know what will happen—tomorrow, a week from now?"

He shrugged.

"Got to be confidential, off the record."

"Then why tell me?"

"Just to give you a break," he said. "The thing is—you asked me—yeah, I've got a client. If anything comes of this, my client won't testify."

I stared at him some more, switched off my desk lamp and reached for my hat.

"Then I don't see any point in discussing it," I said.

"Wait! No reason she'll—my client—ever have to testify. I'm just filling in the picture."

"Then for God's sake, go ahead and fill it in."

"Sure. The night Lorrie King was—killed herself—she had a visitor."

"Who?"

"Guy about thirty years old, good-looking guy, well set up, but on the gay side, you know? A fag."

A pause.

"Well," I said, "is that it?"

113

"Not quite. Happens he was recognized. He's an artist, fellow named Dillon. Byron Dillon."

"What time of day was it?" I asked.

"Night. Evening—around nine o'clock."

"He was seen to enter her apartment, and to leave it?"

"Yeah."

"Who saw him?"

"Can't say."

His hands were nervous now and his eyes showed uncertainty.

"Can you tell me this?" I asked. "How was this witness in a position to observe this arrival and departure?"

He looked at his hands.

"Just happened to be in that position."

"Was it you?" I asked.

He shook his head violently.

"Oh no, not me!"

"Anything observed from inside the apartment?"

"No, just outside."

I thought about it. Not too hard.

"Byron Dillon," I said. "You're sure about the name?"

"Dead sure."

I pretended to think some more.

"All right," I said. "It may be useful. Thanks."

He hung briefly on the edge of the chair, then got up.

"Buy you a drink?" I said.

"Well, you don't have to—"

"I'm on my way out. We can drop in around the corner."

"Okay. Appreciate it."

I got my hat and we went outside. The cold lake breeze hit us and we paused to tighten our hats and shrug into our jackets.

At the bottom of my steps a quick reverse leads on down to a basement storeroom. There aren't any lights down there. Sharkey and I hit the sidewalk together and you couldn't have counted to one and a half before the action was all around us.

There were two of them, big and hard and calculating. I felt myself caught by my jacket front and the back of my neck and slammed down toward the basement. It had been too sudden to get set and I flew halfway down, bounced once and slammed into the brick wall underneath the boarded-up window of the storeroom. It knocked me out.

Within seconds, unhappily, I was living again, with a harsh pain behind my eyes and blood on my chin. Three steps above me the two were beating the sense out of Sharkey. One of them held him from behind while the other worked him over. He was an expert. Sharkey's head was already limp on his shoulders. I tried to get up, to do something, and I couldn't move. By the time I could pull my legs up under me, they had pushed Sharkey down into the stair well and were going away.

I rolled him over and patted his face some, but he was far gone and badly battered. I tried to lift him and get him up the steps, but he was heavy and my own muscles weren't good enough yet to make it. I got up the steps and into my office and called the nearest ambulance service, then took a blanket down and put it over him. I tried again to bring him around, but they had gone at him too hard. He would be laid up for a couple of days.

It was ten minutes before the ambulance arrived. I helped load him on the stretcher and they carried him off.

"Who is he?" one of the attendants asked.

"A guy named Andrew Sharkey," I said.

"Where shall we take him?"

"Some emergency place," I said. "I don't know whether he can pay or not."

"Okay."

They loaded him and took off, opening the siren, and I took my blanket and pulled myself back to the office and into the bathroom. I took a couple of pills, washed myself and changed my suit and shirt. I had a puffed underlip and a bruise on my left temple. My shoulder was twisted and didn't work quite right, but aside from that, I was all right.

On the way out, I paused, thought a minute and picked up the telephone. Pretty soon, Western Union came on.

"A night letter," I said, "to Mr. Edward Rounds, at Carson and Brady, Advertising. Dear Mr. Rounds: Your boys are pretty good. They took care of Sharkey. You can tell Mrs. Rounds he'll be unable to resume work for several days. Don't worry. I'll never tell anyone you were hanging around Lorrie King. She's dead now anyway. I guess we can all forget about it."

I didn't bother to sign it. The girl read it back to me and it was all right and I put on a different hat, went outside and picked up a taxi at Michigan.

I got to Lorrie King's building five minutes early and

went inside to check it out. It was a well-run place, the corridors quiet and glossy and no prying eyes. I rode up to her floor, unlocked the apartment with Dr. Kramm's key and had a look at the place. There was no sign that anyone had been there since I had left the day before. I closed the door and went downstairs to meet Clarissa.

She, too, had come in a taxi and she had a small purse in one hand and an accessory case in the other, such as models carry. It was legitimate. She was, among other things, a model. She was extremely bright and had been a help to me on occasions when a woman's touch was needed. I knew her only professionally, though she was well known around town.

"Nice of you to come," I said, leading her into the lobby.

"Nice to see you again," she said. "How are things?"

"So-so."

"Lead on," she said.

We crossed the lobby and got into an elevator. Clarissa said nothing on the way up. She came along to the door of Lorrie King's apartment and waited while I unlocked it. She started in, stopped, turned back and gave me a look.

"Hey," she said, "isn't this where that society girl— King? Lorrie King?"

"That's right," I said.

"Oh-oh," she said.

After a moment she went on inside and I followed and closed the door.

"I feel like a creep," she said.

"No need," I said. "Everything's cleaned up."

117

She looked the place over.

"Pretty rich, isn't it?" she said.

"A rich girl."

"Yeah."

She found her way to the bedroom, dropped her purse and the case on the bed and looked around some more.

"What's the routine?" she asked.

I went into the bathroom, closed the drain and turned on the water, fooling with it till it seemed to be running a comfortable temperature. Clarissa wandered in and looked into the tub.

"That's where they found her," she said.

"Yes."

Our eyes met. Hers went from puzzled to horror-stricken.

"You want me—to get in—there?" she said.

"Right."

"Just like she did?"

"Well, not exactly like she did."

"Look, Mac, baby, I love you and all, but—"

I leaned down and turned off the water.

"Nobody's going to force you," I said. "It would be a great help to me."

She stared into the clear, greenish water in the tub. I noticed for the first time that the tub itself was of a greenish hue.

"What are you trying to prove?" she said.

"I'm not sure. I've got a kind of an idea."

She stared some more.

"Fifty dollars?" she said.

"Yes."

"How long do I have to stay—in it?"

"About a minute, maybe two."

"Well—"

"You want to test it for hot and cold?"

She frowned at me, frowned at the water in the tub, then slipped out of her right shoe, lifted her skirt, peeled off a stocking and stuck her toes in the water. Lifting them out, she shook her foot daintily, spraying the bathroom floor with minute moisture.

"All right," she said. "Is that all the water you need?"

"No, I'll fill it up."

"You want me stark raw? Can I wear a bikini?"

"Put it this way," I said. "As far as I'm concerned personally, you can wear a bikini or a suit of armor, or anything. But as far as the experiment is concerned, it won't work except on your fundamental skin."

"Oh."

I turned on the water and we stood there while it filled the tub to the overflow outlet. Clarissa picked up her shoe and stocking.

"Okay," she said. "Give me a couple of minutes to get ready. You just want me to get in and sit there?"

"Yup. Call when you're ready. Not too loud."

"Okay."

I went out through the bedroom and waited in the living room. After about a minute and a half I heard her call. I went back to the bathroom and she was sitting in the tub, the water gurgling slowly out the overflow. She was covering herself with her left arm and right hand. Her legs were straight out, her knees locked and her back straight.

"Try and relax," I said. "Lean back against the tub."

She started to lean back, winced and shivered.

"It's cold!"

I sloshed some of the warm water up onto the curving back of the tub to warm it. She tried it again and stayed with it. The water had reached its highest possible level and had stopped overflowing.

"Now let your knees come up," I said. "Easy, just the way they naturally would rise in the water."

She relaxed and her knees rose slowly. She slipped down a little against the back of the tub.

"I'll drown—" she said.

"I won't let you drown. Go ahead—slide down as far as you can, without pushing. Don't brace your feet."

"Like this?"

Her knees rose some more. The cap of her right knee showed just above the surface.

"You're still hanging on," I said. "Let go. Relax."

"You keep saying that. I'm not used to this—"

"All right, it won't be long now."

She took a deep breath, frowned, then relaxed all over. Her hands and forearms floated in the water just under the surface. Both kneecaps showed above the water. Her waist and hips were relaxed. I touched her shoulder, pushing lightly, and she slid down about an inch and a half and stopped.

"That's it?" I said.

"I guess so. I'm relaxed. I'm beginning to enjoy it."

"All right. You can get out now."

Her chin was at least two inches above the surface of the water. She hadn't got her face wet anywhere.

I left the bathroom and was going away through the bedroom when she called,

"Hey, wait—I didn't bring a towel."

I looked back and there weren't any towels hanging in the bathroom. I looked in the linen closet in the dressing room, found a big yellow towel and tossed it to her. She rose in the tub and began to dry herself and I went away to wait for her in the living room.

13

I BOUGHT CLARISSA an eight o'clock dinner and sent her home in a taxi. She was shivering when we left the restaurant and I asked if she thought she had caught a cold.

"Only in my soul," she said. "I never played a bathtub scene in a coffin before."

"I hope never again," I said.

"Good night," she said.

I walked to Byron Dillon's building, went up to his apartment and waited about five minutes for somebody to open the door. Nobody did. By then it was nine-fifteen and I found a taxi and rode back to my office. There was a call from the answering service, from Mulligan, the accountant. I tried to return it, but got no answer. At about twenty minutes to ten a taxi pulled up out front.

I watched through a slit in the window blind as Teresa Russo got out. The taxi pulled away, fast, as if glad to be rid of her. She stood on the sidewalk, looking up at my building. She took something out of her purse, read from it, peering close, looked up again and started toward my front steps. Then she stopped, turned away and walked off down the street toward the lake. I put on my hat, went outside and started after her, not hurrying.

It was a cold night and she walked with her shoulders huddled over her folded arms, her purse dangling at her right elbow. She was wearing a sweater and skirt and her dark hair was clipped at the back of her head and hung around her shoulders.

My office is two blocks from the lake. At the first intersection she stopped and looked in all directions. Off to her right was the old hospital. Along her left were the newer ones, solid, endless walls, punctured here and there by lighted windows. There was a strong wind now and I saw her turn from it, hunching farther forward, and decide against going on to the lake. I waited in the shadow of the hospital entrance, and as she turned back the way she had come, she caught sight of me.

At the first glance there was no recognition and she hurried her pace, getting past me. Then she hesitated, looked around and quickly looked away.

"Teresa—" I said.

She stood where she was, silent.

I gave her some time and moved toward her, not crowding.

"You wanted to see me?" I asked.

She shrugged in her sweater, or shivered, it was hard to tell which.

"Better keep walking," I said. "It's not a good night to stand around."

We started back toward the office. She walked at some distance from me, as if we were separate pedestrians.

"The cop Saunders is giving you a bad time," I said.

"Always," she said. "Always a bad time."

"Why?"

Silence.

"Will you tell me about Lorrie King?" I asked.

More silence. It went on and on. We reached the steps at my building and she stopped.

"This is my office," I said. "Do you want to come in out of the cold?"

She stood there.

"I have to go," she said. "My father will kill me."

"All right. I'll go with you."

"No—"

"Maybe I could help you, if you'd let me," I said. "You must have had some reason to come here. It's a long trip, a long way home."

She straightened then and turned.

"Let's walk some more," she said.

She started off, again toward the lake, and I caught up with her.

"Lorrie—Miss King—" she said, "was the only friend I ever had. She was great. I never knew anybody like her."

More silence.

"When did you first know her?" I asked. "Was it when you were in—pregnant?"

She didn't like the word. She moved away and ahead of me, then slowed.

"No, before," she said. "I—got expelled from school. And that's when—I guess she found out at the school and she came around to see me."

"Why were you expelled?"

She hesitated.

"Oh—I was—got caught. With a boy."

"On the school grounds?"

"Sure."

"The same boy?"

"Yes. So naturally, my father found out I was expelled, and he went after me—"

"He beat you?"

"Sure—he was hitting me, and I was yelling at him, trying to get away, and that's when Miss King came—right in the middle of it."

"What did she do?"

"Well—see, my mother let her in, because, I was, you know, yelling and it might be the police—but it was Miss King. And my mother had a broom in her hand and Miss King grabbed the broom and started hitting my father with it, and he stopped."

Lorrie King, I thought.

"So—that's the first time I saw her."

"And she talked to you? That first time?"

"She took me out and bought me some ice cream and talked to me. My father didn't want to let me go with her, but she told him she could turn him in to the social workers or something, and he let me go."

"And she bought you ice cream and talked to you?"

"She was great—terrific. She didn't really say much. Me—I talked. She never chewed me out or anything, or lectured me. The only thing—she told me she could maybe get me back in school, but not more than once, so I would have to—she said, do my necking somewhere else."

"I see."

"Because if I got kicked out again, they'd send me to the probation or whatever it is."

"You didn't get kicked out of school again?"

"No. I just got—that way."

"And you were scared."

"Naturally. I was scared sick."

"And Miss King helped you again?"

"Yeah—she—I called her up. I had her telephone number. And she came and met me at the ice-cream place."

"What did she say?"

"Well—she said if I would go ahead and have the—baby—she would pay for it and help me."

"You didn't want to do that?"

"Oh God no. I was too scared."

"How did you convince her?"

"I don't know—not right then. I said I'd think about it. And a couple of days later she came again and I was really cracking up then and I cried and yelled and like that and she could see I was serious. And then—"

After a pause, I prompted,

"And then what?"

"My brother got into it."

"Tony?"

"Yeah." She turned her head to look at me. "You knew him?"

"No. I heard about him."

"He's dead—he got in this fight—"

"I know."

"Anyway, he talked to Miss King—two or three times—"

"Excuse me, how did Tony find out about your condition?"

"From my mother."

"You told her?"

"No—but I guess she figured it out. I don't know how."

"But she didn't tell your father?"

"Oh, she would be scared to tell him."

"How did Tony take it?"

"Well, first he was going to kill this—boy. Then I told him he should talk to Miss King, if he wanted to do something sensible. And he did and he told me to do exactly whatever Miss King said, or he'd beat me up."

"But you couldn't do exactly whatever she said."

"No. And I wasn't afraid of Tony, like I am of my father. He didn't scare me."

"Just the baby scared you."

"That's right. So I carried on and did some more yelling and finally Miss King said she'd try to get me fixed."

"And how did she do that?"

"She took me to a doctor—a real doctor. But I can't go into that, because I promised her I wouldn't tell anybody. The rest of my life."

"All right. Tell me this, your brother Tony, did he develop a big thing for Miss King?"

"I guess he did."

"Did he see her a lot?"

"I don't know. I never paid much attention. He never talked about her."

"When did you get the job at Big Danny's store?"

"As soon as school was out. I wasn't going back to school and Miss King said she'd help me get a job. So I got one."

"Did Big Danny know you'd had the trouble?"

"Yes."

"How did he know? Did Miss King tell him?"

"No, she wouldn't ever tell anybody."

"Your brother wouldn't tell him."

"No."

"How would he know?"

She shrugged.

"Big Danny knows everything in the neighborhood. Everything."

"And then Saunders the cop found out."

She looked at me again.

"I guess so. What makes you think so?"

"Only way to explain how he has power over you."

"It's not over me. It's something else."

"What do you think?"

"I don't know. The night Miss King died—or the next day—right after—he came looking for me. He said he had a job for me."

"He was going to pay you?"

"Not exactly. He just said he wanted me to meet somebody and if I didn't do it, he'd make trouble for me."

"You didn't want to do it?"

"No, I didn't want to."

"Did he say whom he wanted you to meet?"

"He just said it was somebody I'd met once before. He said it was a police matter."

"You thought maybe he wanted you to turn stool pigeon?"

"Something like that. Yeah. And besides—I wouldn't

do anything for him. He's a rat. He—that fight my brother got in, when he was killed?"

"Yes."

"That cop saw it. He could have stopped it. But he didn't do a thing. He just watched. And after, he arrested the kid. But Tony was already dead."

We had returned to the intersection and stopped to let some cars pass.

"When is this meeting supposed to take place?"

"He said he'd let me know," she said. "Maybe tomorrow."

We crossed the street and started past the hospital toward my office.

"I told you last night," I said, "I had a job for you too."

"Well?"

"How about it?"

"What do you want me to do?"

"Nothing you're not prepared for. I just want you to go along with the cop, to this meeting."

"Well—what?"

"Just go along and do whatever he wants—I mean, anything you can do safely—and pretend you're willing. Be cooperative."

"What will you do?"

"I'll be around, watching. You'll be safe enough."

"But I—I don't know—"

"Listen," I said. "You came to see me tonight to see if I could help you get away from the cop Saunders, right?"

"Something like that—"

"I'm glad you came. If you'll go along, the way I've told you, I promise you he won't ever bother you again."

Silence.

"What's it about?" she asked.

"I don't know all the details. Even if I did, I wouldn't tell you. I don't want you to be self-conscious about it."

"But what—"

"You can figure on this: The sergeant needs you. He doesn't want any harm to come to you, because you're important to his plans. Besides this, if you'll go along with it, do just what he says, I'll be somewhere close all the time, and I'll see that nothing bad happens to you."

We were back in front of the office again. She stood there with her shoulders hunched, her chin down in her collar.

"Do you want to come in, have some coffee, before you go home?" I asked.

She looked up at my lighted window and shook her head.

"No. I got to go. My father will kill me."

"I'll have to go in to call you a taxi."

"You don't have to. Somebody's coming for me."

"Oh."

"What time is it?"

"Ten-twenty," I said.

"Twenty minutes after ten?"

"Yes."

"Any minute now."

"If I'm not too nosy," I said, "who's coming?"

"Big Danny—I mean, he's sending for me."

"I see. Big Danny knew you were coming to see me?"

"Sure. I wouldn't know where you lived or anything. How would I know? I asked Big Danny."

"Uh-huh. And Big Danny sent Dingo."

"I guess so."

"What reason did you give Big Danny for wanting to see me?"

"Oh, I just said I wanted to see you about Tony."

"Your brother?"

"Yeah. I said I thought maybe there was more than just that one kid—like they were bugging Tony just before the fight, a whole gang of them, and—you being a detective—maybe you could figure out what really happened."

"But that was just the story you told Big Danny."

"Yeah. See, I know what really happened all right. This kid happened to find out about me and—the trouble, and who did it—this other kid. And he was giving Tony a bad time about it. And Tony is quick-tempered, so he got in the fight—and he got killed."

"And Big Danny went for your story all right?"

"Sure. Big Danny is interested in the neighborhood, you know. He wants everything to be taken care of all the time, and if anybody's in trouble, he wants to know all about it and what—to fix it up. You know."

"I guess so."

She drew her shoulders tight and shivered in the cold.

"When you told Big Danny about wanting to see me about Tony," I said, "did he go for it right away, or did he ask you to wait awhile?"

"Well, I was working in the store and I told him about it, and he said I should go back to work and he'd see me later and—like that."

"And then later he saw you and said he'd fix it up for you to come and see me."

"Yeah."

"So you got here, in the taxi—but you didn't come in. Why was that?"

"By the time I got here, I thought the whole thing was silly. You wouldn't be interested in Tony anyway, and besides I didn't really know anything about you. So I chickened out."

"All right. What are you going to tell Big Danny when you get back? About seeing me about Tony?"

She shrugged.

"I'll think of something."

"Maybe you ought to think of something now, so you'll be ready."

"Like what?" she said.

"Maybe like this: You came and told me about the fight Tony got in. You thought there was more behind it than just the one kid. And we talked about it and I told you—and this is the important thing to remember—I told you that even if there was something more behind it, Sergeant Saunders had made an arrest and it was his case. If I started fooling around with it, I'd get in trouble with the police and I already had trouble with Sergeant Saunders—as Big Danny knows you know, because you were there and saw it happen. So there wasn't anything I could do about it. You might say that I suggested that if you wanted to look into it further, you could go to the police yourself—starting with Sergeant Saunders."

"Okay," she said.

"You'll remember that all right?"

"I guess so."

"That is what I would tell Big Danny if I were you."

"All right. I'll tell him—if he asks me."

"I think, in all likelihood, he will ask you."

A big car came fast off Michigan Avenue, made a U-turn in the dead-end street across from my office, and pulled up, some distance from the curb. It was the Cadillac I had seen parked behind Big Danny's store. As it came to a stop, I made out Dingo in the front seat on the curb side. The driver was lanky and thin. I couldn't see anyone in the back.

"I guess this is your ride," I said to Teresa.

"Yeah, it looks like it."

"You remember what I suggested?"

"I remember."

"Just remember to go along with the sergeant and I'll see that no harm comes to you."

"If you say so."

"Better get in now."

"All right."

I walked over to the car with her. Dingo twisted in his seat to unlock the back door. A close look persuaded me the back seat was empty. I helped Teresa in and closed the door.

"Drive carefully," I said to Dingo.

He shrugged in that twitchy way. The car pulled away fast, as it had come. I stood looking after it for a minute, then went to my own car, got it started and pulled away.

I didn't try to keep up with Big Danny's car, but drove fast enough to make the neighborhood on time. At about eleven o'clock I pulled up on the side street just off the alley to Danny's back lot. I left the car, walked away up the street and waited. After about five minutes the big car swished around the corner, swinging wide, turned into the alley and disappeared. I walked down that way and watched Dingo and the driver get out, followed by Teresa from the back seat. The three of them went into the back entrance of the store.

Could be, I said, she came on orders. Could be she's spying for Saunders and Big Danny.

But I didn't think so.

But it might be. She got cold feet when she arrived and that's why she didn't come in.

But what could they want by way of intelligence? They knew my client. They knew my interest in Lorrie King. What else did they know?

There was nothing else they could know.

I waited, pacing now and then to keep my circulation going against the cold. It was twenty minutes before Teresa emerged from the back entrance, made her way on foot along the alley, and turned toward the main street and home. I gave her a good lead, then went after her. I watched her make the three-block walk to her tenement and turn in. I moved up then, and there was nobody loitering in the entrance. I saw her legs disappearing up the stairs.

She's all right, I decided. She's home safe and, aside from a chewing out from her father, she will be all right the rest of the night.

There was nothing more I could do about it anyway. If I could hang around the whole night, I couldn't cover the tenement entirely. Besides, there were other things to be done.

I walked down the street, past Big Danny's store, and went into the phone booth. I dialed Mulligan's number, and after about six rings he came on.

"Sorry if I got you out of bed," I said.

"All right," he said grumpily. "You want a report, come on over to my place."

"You've got everything?"

"I got some things."

"About half an hour?"

"Okay."

I left the phone and walked back to the car. Heading for the South Side, where Mulligan lived, I wondered again,

What could they want to know? What is there to know?

14

MULLIGAN HAD a gentleman's flat on the South Side, on the fringe of Jackson Park. It had once been a nice place to live, but now it was run-down in about the same proportion as Mulligan himself. But run-down or not, he had a shrewdness and tenacity that only age can bring. When he showed you an object, you knew it was real.

He was in pajamas and a bathrobe and slippers and he moved lumpily around his cluttered living room, like a sack loosely filled with potatoes. He opened a finger-marked manila folder on a card table and showed me what he had.

"The King girl was tough," he said. "All I could get was that she had made certain withdrawals from a special account at certain dates. Substantial withdrawals, like ten grand here, fifteen there."

"You've pinned down the dates?"

"Yeah. It's all written out here."

"That was all you could get on her?"

"That's it. She was worth about two million in her own right, when she died."

"You don't have any payouts to correspond to the withdrawals?"

He looked at me as if I were from another planet.

"Where in hell would I be able to get that? With her dead?"

"I don't know. Sorry I asked."

He snorted, cleared his throat and offered me a drink. I declined. He poured a slug of bourbon for himself and turned to another pile of papers in the folder.

"The guy Saunders is still alive and I got more on him."

"Like what?"

He began to show me and it was beautiful, the way it must be in the mind of a chess player when he visualizes the end game and knows he can't lose. It was all there, in written records, including photostats of bank statements. It was what I had come to expect of Mulligan.

"I'll have that drink now," I said, when he had finished. "If you have the time."

"Why not?" he said.

He poured me a drink and we sat with it, mostly in silence.

"Am I going to have to testify to any of this?" he asked.

"Very possible," I said.

He sighed.

"You're a good witness," I said. "I like to think of you being on there."

He grimaced.

"How much do I owe you?" I asked.

"Hundred and fifty," he said.

"Cash or check?"

"Always check. I'm a methodical person."

He always said the same thing and I always asked the same question. It was a ritual between us.

I made out a check for him for a hundred and fifty, said good night and left.

I got home at one-fifteen in the morning, got undressed and into bed and picked up the phone. My answering service said there had been calls ever since midnight at ten-minute intervals. A Dr. Kramm. I should call him. Urgent.

I found his number and dialed. He came right on.

"Right after midnight," he said, "I got a call from somebody who wouldn't give me his name. He said it was important to me and to the memory of Lorrie that we get together. I have no idea who he is or what he has to say or anything."

"Did he set up a meeting place?"

"No. He said he'd let me know later."

"Did he set a time?"

"No. He'll call me about that too."

"He didn't give you any idea what he wants to see you about?"

"No. He only said it's important to my career—whatever the hell that means."

It means a lot, I thought. It means everything.

I lay there with the phone, trying to decide. If it had been only for myself—one thing. But it was for him and his career, whatever that meant.

Well, I thought, go for broke. Take the big one. It can be worked out, I think. And besides, he sure as hell asked for it.

"I advise you to go ahead, go along with him," I said. "But keep in close touch with me."

"I'll try."

"I'll get your calls any hour, any time. I'll check with

my answering service every fifteen minutes and if I hear from you, I'll call right back."

"You have any idea what this is about?"

"No," I said. "But if we don't go along now, we'll never know."

"All right," he said. "But keep in touch."

"Guaranteed."

"Thanks. Good night."

There were no other calls to be made. Nothing left but to go to sleep. It would be difficult but maybe possible. I could try.

I tried for about an hour and a half, then got up, took a couple of pills and went back. They worked. I didn't wake up till the middle of the next morning.

Before I even got out of bed, I started putting in calls to a lawyer named Joe Briggs. He was one of the county's most competent deputies and I had known him for a long time. I knew he had more discretionary responsibility than anyone else in the department except the boss himself. I kept the call working while I shaved and dressed and finally got hold of him about eleven-fifteen.

"Got a hot one for you," I said. "When can we talk?"

"Tomorrow morning?" he said.

"Too late."

"Hang on."

I could hear him muttering about appointments, lunch with the boss. Finally he came back.

"Best I can do is three-twenty this afternoon."

"It's tight," I said, "but it will have to do."

We agreed on a spot to meet and I hung up.

I grabbed a fast cup of coffee at Tony's joint, got in my car and drove out to Big Danny's neighborhood. By day it was teeming, raucous, and it smelled bad. Without the softening dark and masking lights, Big Danny's store front was a drab expanse of glass and brick.

At the birdseed counter a clerk I hadn't seen before asked what I wanted. I bought a package of birdseed.

"There was a young lady working here last night—" I said.

"You must mean the Russo girl," she said down her nose.

"I don't know her name. We had a slight argument over a purchase. I wanted to apologize."

"She only works a half shift today," she said. "Twelve-thirty to five-thirty."

My watch read twelve-ten. I thanked her, went outside, dropped the birdseed in a trash can and wandered up the street to wait. At twelve thirty-five I went back to the store. The clerk who had waited on me wasn't there and I confronted a large-bosomed lady with a pair of glasses on a chain. She kept putting them on and letting them fall to the end of the chain so that they bounced against her chest.

"Young lady named Russo works here," I said. "I hoped I could see her for a minute."

The lady frowned and the glasses fell.

"She phoned in, she's sick and can't come to work," she said. "That's why I'm here. I work at the jewelry counter, but they put me over here in the bird department because Miss Russo doesn't feel well. I don't know

140

anything about birds—I hate birds—"

"Yes, ma'am," I said.

I left the store again at twelve forty-five. I would have to make it all the way to the Loop by three-twenty and there wasn't much spread.

Saunders will be watching the Russo apartment, I thought. He doesn't want anything to go wrong now.

I found a phone booth and looked up the Russos, but there was no listing.

If she's sick, I thought, and the whole thing is off—but I doubt that Saunders would put up with her being sick.

I walked up the street to the cigar store where the kids had been hanging out the night before. There were three or four of them in the place now and the sounds were daylight sounds and different from those of the night. The proprietor, in shirt sleeves, wearing dark glasses, was sitting on a stool behind the cash register. I bought a couple of cigars and broke out a twenty-dollar bill.

"I need a dependable kid to run an errand," I said. "Take a few minutes. Five dollars."

He went ahead and made my change, then shrugged. "What's dependable?"

"Very simple errand. Nothing wrong with it. Go down the street a few doors and come back."

He leaned across the glass-topped counter and called, "Hey, Gino!"

I couldn't tell who he was looking at with the glasses. Gino turned out to be a husky teen-ager with a permanent scowl and a bad left hand, crippled by polio.

"Want a quick job?" the proprietor said.

"What kind of a job?"

"Few minutes. Five bucks."

"What do I have to do?"

The proprietor waved toward me and retired. Gino looked at me from a distance.

"What do you want?"

"You know Teresa Russo?"

"Who doesn't?" he said.

"Where she lives?"

"Yeah, sure, I know."

"I want you to go up to her place and tell her I want to see her."

"Who shall I say?"

"Her uncle. Uncle Mac."

He studied me briefly, leered and held out his hand. "Five? Okay."

"When you get back," I said.

He studied me some more, shrugged and went out. I stood by the counter waiting. He was gone about five minutes and returned shrugging.

"She ain't home," he said.

"Did they say where she is?"

He held out his good hand.

"I went up there, okay? Five?" he said.

"Did they say where she is?"

He gestured impatiently with his bad hand.

"At work. She works. Big Danny's. She went to work."

I found a five-dollar bill and handed it to him. He snaked it into his pocket and walked away.

She could be there at the store all right, it occurred to

me, without being at work. She could be downstairs there, on ice.

I walked over to where the boy Gino was bulling with his friends and pulled at his sleeve. He turned impatiently.

"Another five bucks?" I said.

"For what?"

"Danny's store. I'll write a message. Just be sure you hand it to Big Danny himself."

He studied me with the leer big on his face now.

"Man, you're really hot for her, huh?" he said.

"Five bucks to take the message," I said.

"Okay, what the hell."

I found a scrap of paper and scrawled a message to Big Danny:

"Send the Russo kid up to her regular counter. I want to talk to her—no time to go downstairs. Saunders."

I folded the paper and handed it to Gino. It wasn't a very believable message. I would have to take the chance that Saunders might be on duty and would have a logical reason to get in and out of the store in a hurry.

"I'll go down to the store with you," I said. "I'll give you the five when you go in. Just hand the paper to Big Danny and cut out."

He shrugged and started out. I caught up with him and we walked down the street to the store. In the doorway I handed him another five and watched him move away toward the staircase and Danny's platform station. Then I walked away up the street, loitered briefly and wandered back to the entrance. I hovered there for a few minutes and Teresa didn't appear at the birdseed counter. I looked at my watch and it was something after one o'clock.

I took another short walk up the street and back and looked in and she was coming from the back room into the bird department. The saleslady with the glasses appeared to be chewing her out. Teresa stood with her head down, taking it. I moved toward the counter slowly. The lady was still talking when I reached it. Teresa glanced past her and caught sight of me. I beckoned and she looked helplessly at me, turned her head as if to escape the barrage of words, then stuck out her chin and said,

"All right! Shut up! I've got to take care of a customer."

The saleslady, still talking, stalked off. Teresa came to the counter.

"What do you want?" she said.

"Listen," I said, "I've only got a minute. Don't tell Big Danny I was here."

"Okay. What?"

"Saunders has some kind of arrangement with you, for this evening," I said.

"Yeah. How did you—?"

"Never mind. All I want to know is what time?"

"He said he'd pick me up here at six-thirty."

"Six-thirty. Okay. That's all I need. Thanks."

"Listen—" she said as I turned away.

"You'll be all right," I said. "Just go along with him."

"Well—"

"Believe me," I said, and left her quickly.

It was close to one-thirty when I got to my car and

headed downtown. I hadn't had anything to eat except coffee and my stomach churned all the way. It was slow going but I pushed the traffic hard and made it to the coffee shop where Joe Briggs had agreed to meet me in time to order a ham sandwich. Joe came in as it was being served and I ordered a cup of coffee for him.

"Talk fast," he said. "I got a bad day."

"You've got a bad cop," I said.

"Which?" he said. "I mean, who?"

"Saunders," I said. "Clay Saunders, detective."

He drank some coffee and was silent long enough to show he knew a little. Then he said,

"Well?"

"I think I've got him for you. Packaged. Ready for delivery."

"For what?"

"Blackmail."

He winced.

"Attempted?" he said.

"Accomplished," I said. "Collected."

"Past or present?"

"Both."

He sat with his hands flat on the table, staring into the cup. Then he picked it up, went through the line and came back with a refill. I had my scraps of evidence out of my pockets by the time he came back and I laid them out for him. Reluctantly at first, then with growing interest, he examined them one by one, holding each up for my interpretation.

"Safe-deposit box number," I said. "Western Commercial on Ashland Avenue." Then, "Statements showing deposits in checking account over a two-year period. More deposits than a cop can save up in ten years. A different bank." Then, "Another checking account in another bank, ordinary, right on the verge of overdraft, like a cop might have." Then, "Photograph of a young girl named Teresa Russo." Next, "Notes left by his victim—dates, times and places of rendezvous." Last, "Photograph of a dead woman in a bathtub."

He looked at the photo for some time, put it down gently and looked at me for a longer time.

"Lorrie King," he said. "She's dead. What have you got that's fresh?"

"Tonight at seven o'clock," I said. *"Flagrante delicto."*

"Who's involved?"

"My client."

He sighed, drank some more coffee, looked again at the evidence.

"What's your deal?" he asked.

"Immunity for my client."

I was far out now. We both knew that he could turn me down, put a tail on Saunders and collect his own evidence and the hell with any immunity. But we both knew, too, that my evidence would help, and that it was necessary for us to live together one way or another.

"Let me hear it," he said.

"It was an illegal operation. About two years ago. My client was the doctor. The patient was the Russo girl, who is alive and well. Miss King was involved and she paid off to Saunders until she died. Now he's after the doctor. I've advised my client to go ahead and meet him. I plan to be there."

146

He put both hands over his face and rubbed it hard. When he took them away, he was grinning one-sidedly.

"And I have the rare privilege of being there too—provided the doctor gets immunity."

"That is correct."

He thought about it, not for long.

"If we can do it on the earlier evidence," he said. "But if we can't—if we have to call the doctor?"

"You'll find a way. The girl is all right. She's not going to bring any charges. Miss King is dead."

"What's the alternative?" he asked.

I shrugged and picked up my papers.

"I'll have to handle it my own way and hope nobody gets hurt—prematurely."

He looked at me some more, not smiling.

"Goddam you," he said softly. "Listen—even if we let him off the hook, they'll take his license."

"Not necessarily. Even if he has to testify, you can handle it so he doesn't acknowledge a thing except that Saunders put it up to him."

"Defense will call the girl."

"Maybe," I said, "but I don't think that will mean a thing."

"You fairly sure of that?"

"I'm very damn sure."

"What time do we have to leave?"

"From downtown about four forty-five."

"You sure you can pick Saunders up?"

"I'm sure. He's got the girl stashed and he's picking her up at six-thirty. At a store out on the West Side. Big Danny's."

Joe made a bad face.

"There's one—" he said.

"Later," I said. "Now just Saunders."

"Your car or mine?" he said.

"Not mine. Saunders knows mine."

He gave it a full, long, solid minute. And then he nodded once.

"Okay. I'll pick you up on the corner here at a quarter to five."

"I'll be there," I said. "You won't regret it. I'll have something better even, when Saunders is in the bag."

We were getting up and he paused, bent, gorilla-like, both hands on the table.

"Better what?"

"Lorrie King," I said.

"What about Lorrie King?"

"She was murdered," I said.

We got up all the way and walked out of the place.

15

At five-thirty it began to rain. By six the rain was a steady downpour and it was cold, even inside Joe Briggs's tight, late-model Chevy. He was a good driver, but I had begun to clench my fists from time to time against the fear we might make Big Danny's store too late.

Then at six-fifteen we cut through the warehouse alley and Danny's big lights blinked on and off at us dead ahead. I told Joe how to make the turns. The street was busy and this took some time, and also provided cover.

"You have any kind of insignia on this thing?" I asked.

"No," Joe said. "It's all mine."

We turned right onto the side street and drifted past the alley that led to the rear of the Big Store. Joe went on some thirty yards and pulled to the curb. I got out, turned up my coat collar and slogged back to the alley, turned in there and reached the back of the store. Three cars were parked there and Saunders' was not among them. I had to figure he might use another for tonight, but the chances were against it.

I had turned to leave when headlights flared on the street, swerved and brightened. I ducked behind the nearest car and waited. A late-model inexpensive sedan swung into the alley, rolled into the first open slot, and the lights went out. The door slammed. I moved around the screening car and watched Saunders walk into the service area of the store, moving fast, not looking around. He disappeared and I went back to the side street.

Joe had turned the car around and was parked on the opposite side, some distance back from the alley. I opened the far door and looked in at him.

"There's no other way out," I said. "He has to come out this way. I'm going to phone."

He looked at his watch.

"The one just drove in?" he said.

"Yeah. I watched him get out."

"Okay," he said. "Hurry it."

I closed the door, ran to the corner and turned right. There was a phone booth about twenty yards along, against the wall of a liquor store. I went in there and dialed the doctor's home number. As it began to ring, Teresa Russo walked past, not hurrying, wearing a drab raincoat, her shoulders hunched, a small bag swinging at her side.

They're pretty sure of her now, I thought. They let her go home.

The phone opened loudly at the other end.

"Yes?" Dr. Kramm said.

"Mac," I said. "Have you had the call?"

"Oh yes—about five minutes ago. He said to meet him at the site of the new Sheridan North Hotel. There's a construction shack, he said, on the north side of the lot."

"What time?"

"Seven. Listen, where are you?"

"I'm not far off."

"I don't like this. Why can't you go with me?"

"Because if I'm there, he'll just walk away. I'll be there, but you won't see me."

"I don't get it—all the secrecy—"

"He's a wrong cop," I said. "He's got something and he wants something in return. We have to know what."

"All right, but—"

"Keep the date. I'll be there. I've got to hang up now."

"Yes. All right—"

I hung up and got out of the booth and returned to Joe's car at a trot. I opened the door and reached for the tape recorder, a miniature that fitted in my coat pocket.

"Got a break," I said. "The doctor got the call. New Sheridan North Hotel, construction shack. I'll take the recorder and a taxi, try to get there first. You follow Saunders, in case of a change, all right?"

"Yeah. Listen—"

"Yeah."

"We got to remember the girl. If we brace him and she's there, he'll go for her. She's his worst witness."

"I know. I'll watch it."

"You watch the girl, I'll watch Saunders, right?"

"Right. Hang on."

I closed the door, trotted back to the main street and walked about half a block. A taxi pulled in and discharged a fare. I slid into the back seat while the driver was collecting.

"Listen," the driver said, "I got to get something to eat. I been on since—"

"I'm in a hurry," I said. "It's worth twenty dollars to me to get to the Sheridan North Hotel."

I handed him a twenty.

"That's different," he said.

He drove a couple of blocks, looping to get headed east.

"Hey," he said. "The Sheridan North—it ain't even up yet."

"I know."

He shrugged and attended to his driving.

By the time we hit the North Side the rain had let up, but the traffic was heavy and slow and it was a drag. We reached the lot where they were building the new hotel at five minutes to seven. I told him to drive all the way around it slowly.

"How else?" he grumbled.

He made the circuit and I saw no familiar cars parked in the vicinity. At the construction shack I asked to be let out.

"Anything else?" he asked.

"No—just go," I said.

He went. I carried the recorder into the shelter of the construction shack and opened the case. It took me three or four seconds to get it running. I had never used one just like it. But when I checked it out, testing, it worked all right. I erased the test, set the tape to go and looked for a place to put it.

The door of the shack was locked and I doubted that Saunders would go so far as to break in, merely to get inside. The rain was intermittent now and there was some overhang along the front side of the shack, where an area had been kept clear of stacked lumber and plasterboard. The nearest pile of material was some twenty feet away, too far for the small recorder. Anyway, I couldn't predict that Saunders would make his pitch under the overhang.

I went on around the shack and saw the looming steel and concrete framework of the new building and what looked like endless piles of building material. Some distance away stood two portable rest rooms. They were good for nothing but to run to.

I decided that if the shack was the firm place for the meeting, I would be better off near it than away from it. There were windows only on one side. I could move around it when necessary.

I made a circuit, checking the ground and the footing. A couple of tin cans had been thrown down near the far end wall and I picked them up and carried them out of the way. At one corner, on the back side, stood an oil drum. I marked its position and went on around. The path was clear all the way, except for the drum, and it was big enough to remember.

I got to thinking. Ordinarily there would be a watchman on a job like this. I had seen no sign of one. Why did Saunders pick this spot? I wondered. How did he know there wouldn't be a watchman?

On the side street nearest the shack a car pulled to the curb. Its lights went dark and a man got out on the far side. He came around and opened the curb door, and a girl got out. Saunders and Teresa Russo. They walked, some distance apart, in a direct line, diagonally from the car toward the shack. I stood near the oil drum, hidden by the end wall, and waited. Saunders surely would check out the place to make sure it was clear. That meant he would probably make a complete turn around the shack, as I had done. With the recorder in one hand and the mike in the other, I would have to move around with him and stay out of sight. If he made the girl help him, if they split and made the rounds in opposite directions, I was dead. But I doubted that he would trust her that far.

Joe Briggs is somewhere on this lot, I thought. I wonder where.

Saunders had taken the girl's hand now, as if to keep her from running away. That was all to the good. They approached by the corner opposite the oil drum and disappeared from my view. Listening, I could hear occasional shuffling footsteps.

"Come on," Saunders said, "we'll take a walk around the shack."

"What for?" Teresa said.

"Come on," he said.

"Listen—"

"Just come on!"

I heard the footsteps again, but it was a hair-raising length of time before I could detect the direction they were taking. I finally placed them as off to my right, and managed to get around the drum and along the back wall ahead of them. I paused once to make sure they were coming on, then went on around the far end. Looking along the front wall, where the windows were, I was in time to see the girl's back disappearing around the corner toward the oil drum. As I started after them, another car stopped on the street, a door opened and slammed shut.

I moved fast along the front wall to the corner, and when I looked around, they were out of sight. I slid in close to the wall, working slowly toward the oil drum.

"Okay," Saunders said, "we'll wait right here."

The voice was clear enough, even from the far side of the shack. I hoped the mike was sensitive and far-reaching.

Standing near the oil drum, I watched Dr. Kramm cross the corner of the lot toward the shack. Fifty feet from it he stopped, looked around, then came on slowly. I set the recorder on the top of the drum and switched it on, then carried the mike as far as the cord would reach toward the front side. I got about halfway along the wall. There was nothing to hang it on and I stood and held it, high up by my shoulder. It swung gently at the end of a length of cord.

"Right here, Doctor," Saunders said.

"Saunders?" Kramm said.

"That's right."

A small, pale flash of light shone, went off, as if Saunders had used an identifying flashlight.

"What is it?" Kramm said.

"Like you to meet a young lady," Saunders said. "This is—"

Kramm cut in, impatient and tense.

"You said you had information about Lorrie King—about her suicide."

"Yeah," Saunders said. "Well, this is about Lorrie King too. First—meet Miss Teresa Russo."

"Well—" Kramm said. "Hello, Miss Russo."

"Hello," she said.

"I don't understand—" Kramm said.

"Come on, Doctor, you've seen Miss Russo before."
Silence.

"Teresa," Saunders said, "you've met the doctor before, haven't you?"
Silence.

"Well—" Saunders pushed, "when did you meet the doctor before?"

"I—don't know."

"Teresa—"

"Listen," Kramm said, "I don't know what you're doing here, or why I'm here. But let's get down to the subject."

"I'm on the subject," Saunders said. "Maybe I need to refresh a couple memories. About two years ago, Doctor, two and a month maybe, Miss Russo here was in a kind of trouble—female trouble."

Silence. I held the mike out as far as I could stretch it. I felt it tug lightly at the recorder and held back in time.

"You remember that, don't you, Teresa? You were knocked—you were going to have a baby."

"Now wait—" Kramm said harshly.

"And Miss Lorrie King knew about it, didn't she, Teresa?"
Silence.

"Miss King knew, didn't she?"

"Yes," Teresa said in a low voice.

"And she said she would help you, didn't she?"

"Yes."

"And she took you to a doctor, is that right?"

"I guess—yes—"

"And the doctor did a kind of operation on you and that took care of the baby. Right?"

Silence.

"Teresa—?"

"Yes," she said.

Kramm's voice was hard and edgy as a saw.

"Saunders, I could kill you—"

"Sure," Saunders said. "But you won't. Not now. Not here."

"What do you want from me?"

The mike hung still as a dead man's hand now.

Saunders declined the question.

"I just want to establish the facts, Doctor," he said. "The doctor that did the operation on Teresa here was you."

"I never saw—!" Kramm said.

"Maybe you can't tell by her face," Saunders said. "Teresa—wasn't this the doctor, the friend of Miss King's, who did that operation on you?"

Silence. Then Teresa gasped lightly, as if he had begun twisting her arm.

"Don't—!" she said. "I don't know—"

"You don't know?" Saunders said.

"Maybe—I don't—I guess it was—"

"Teresa!" Kramm said. "How can you say it?"

"Was it?" Saunders said.

"Yes," Teresa said. "Yes, it was."

"No!" Kramm said. "You can't say that—how could you know? You were blindfolded!"

Silence. Interminable. I imagined I could hear the faint whirring of the tape on the recorder.

"Teresa," Saunders said, "go back to the car."

"No, I—"

"Get going!"

There was a scraping sound, a light thudding as if Saunders had pushed her and she was trying to stay on her feet. The mike swung in my hand, but I stayed with it, holding it. I heard her walk away a few steps and the sound faded.

"What do you want, Saunders?" Kramm said.

It was Saunders' turn to delay, let him sweat.

"Well," he said slowly, "it's like this. It was a long time ago and the girl's all right. I got nothing personal about it. Of course, it's my duty as a law officer to turn you in."

Kramm kept quiet.

"I'd hate to do it," Saunders said. "I like the girl. I'd hate to put her and her family through a thing. And I've got nothing against you." A pause.

"How much?" Kramm said. "How much do you want?"

"Oh, now," Saunders said. "I'm not—"

"How goddam much?" Kramm said, his voice rising suddenly.

"I don't know," Saunders said. "What's a doctor's career worth? A million? Million and a half?"

"You're out of your mind."

"No—but I'm not greedy. I'm not even hungry. How

about, say, twenty thousand—in four payments—five grand each?"

"Cash," Kramm said.

"Yeah, I guess it would have to be."

"I haven't got it with me, naturally."

"Naturally. No hurry. Next couple of days."

"Where?"

"I'll get in touch with you."

Silence.

"You son of a bitch," Kramm said. "You lousy, crummy, two-bit—"

"Knock it off," Saunders said. "I've been named before by better than you."

"Is that all now?" Kramm said.

"That's all."

Gently, as if it were an egg suspended on a thread, I carried the mike to the oil drum, tiptoeing. At the drum I looked around the corner toward the street. Teresa had not returned to the car. She was quite near the shack, leaning against a pile of lumber, her face in her hands. Beyond her, at the end of the lumber pile, a man's hat appeared, then slowly the rest of him. Joe Briggs.

I heard footsteps, moving away. I watched until I had made sure it was Kramm, heading for the street and his car. I moved along the back wall toward Teresa as Joe Briggs ducked out of sight to let the doctor pass. At the corner of the shack I stopped, listening. There were more footsteps. Saunders walked away toward the street, toward Teresa. I got my gun out and moved into line behind him. He was halfway to where Teresa waited when I called him.

"Hold it, Saunders."

He wheeled, ducking, and his hand went to his jacket. I caught a glimpse of Joe Briggs coming fast from the lumber pile, past Teresa. I made it to the shelter of the back wall as Saunders blasted at me. The slug hit the shack, cracking. Joe Briggs was in a direct line of fire between Saunders and the girl. Saunders looked that way and leveled the gun. I let one go at him, low into the ground. It hit very close and he fell to one side. Briggs had no gun.

"Run, Teresa!" I yelled at her.

"Give up, Saunders," Briggs said.

He was standing broadside to Saunders, who leaned on one elbow on the ground, his gun in his hand.

"Drop it, Saunders," I said.

I stepped around the corner into view, letting him see the gun. He swung onto his knees, his arm coming around to let me have it. Joe rushed him. They went down and became one writhing clump. I ran over there and Saunders was wrestling, trying to get Joe on the head with the barrel of his gun. I got hold of his wrist, twisting, and he dropped it. He kicked up once at Joe and I twisted again and he gave up. He crumpled onto one side with his fingers clawing at the dirt and put his head down. I picked up his gun, handed it to Briggs and nudged Saunders with my foot.

"Get up now," I said.

It had begun to rain again. Saunders raised himself slowly and there was mud on the side of his face. Briggs pulled handcuffs from his pocket. I handed him my gun and put the shackles on Saunders, who made no move to resist. Briggs gave my gun back to me and put the other in his pocket.

"This way, Saunders," he said.

"You want me to ride with you?" I asked.

"No," Briggs said. "I'll call in and wait for help. Look after the girl."

"The recorder," I said.

Briggs gave me a one-sided grin.

"Oh, yeah, come to think of it," he said.

"I'll get it."

I ran to the oil drum and the tape was still running. I switched the thing off, coiled the mike line and left the shack. By the time I caught up with Briggs and Saunders, they were at the street. Briggs's car was parked about thirty yards behind Saunders'. I walked down there behind them and Briggs opened the rear door and put Saunders inside. I opened the front door and laid the recorder carefully on the floor, out of reach in case Saunders should lunge for it.

"That do it for now?" I said.

"For now," Briggs said. "Thanks. Call me in the morning early."

"Yeah," I said.

I walked back along the street to where Teresa Russo stood, leaning against Saunders' car, her body slumped, the purse dangling from her right hand, her eyes staring.

"If you can walk with me a little," I said, "I'll find a taxi to take you home."

She didn't say anything. After a moment I touched

her arm and she moved from the car and came along. We walked the dark side street toward a main north-south thoroughfare.

"I don't know how to make it believable to you," I said, "but everything will be all right. With you and with the doctor."

Silence. Her small handbag banged lightly against my thigh.

"Thanks for going along with us," I said. "You're a brave girl."

"It's all right," she said.

"What will they do to the cop—Saunders?" she asked after a while.

"They'll put him away good."

"What about when he gets out?"

"We'll see that you're protected," I said.

She didn't say anything to that. She knew as well as I, it was a dubious promise.

There was a cabstand about three blocks down from the construction job. One cab was waiting. I put Teresa in it, gave the driver ten dollars and told him where to go.

"Good night," I said. "Don't worry."

She looked at me and looked away.

"Yeah," she said.

The cab pulled away. I stood in the rain for about ten minutes and another pulled up. I got in and directed the driver to Dr. Kramm's apartment.

16

I RANG THE DOORBELL SIX times before he would open up. I knew he was there; I had checked to make sure his car was in the garage and I had seen there were lights in his apartment.

"Oh—" he said. "It's you."

He turned his back on me and walked away into the bedroom. He was in his shirt sleeves and slippers and after I had closed the door I gave him a couple of minutes to collect himself. When I went into the bedroom, he was sitting on the bed, brooding up at the portrait of Lorrie King. There was no reading him—not that I tried.

I waited. He got up, went to the bathroom, drew himself a drink of water and returned to sit on the bed.

"You must have set it up," he said. "Why?"

"You'll have to believe what you can," I said. "It would have happened; Saunders knew about it. I tried to set it up so we could control it."

"Control it," he said. "Twenty thousand dollars. All right. For now. And pretty soon again—another twenty thousand? What the hell do you mean, control?"

"Saunders won't collect from you. Saunders won't be available for years to come. He's in custody now."

He said nothing for a while.

"How did you arrange that?" he said.

"I had a thing going with the law."

"Oh, great."

"In return for a promise of immunity for you, I got to set the thing up and do it my way. And they've got Saunders."

He was looking at me now, still distant, still unbelieving, but listening.

"Immunity?" he said. "How?"

"Saunders will go on trial. They've got evidence on previous blackmail, collected. They've got other stuff on him, stuff they couldn't hope to nail him with without this other. You'll be called to testify. The prosecution will see to it you don't have to acknowledge anything except that you met Saunders and he put it up to you."

"The girl will testify too."

"The girl was blindfolded. Saunders' lawyer won't even fool with it. He'll pass. All he can hope for is to get Saunders off as light as possible. If he tries to destroy a reputable medical doctor, the jury will kill him. The only witness against you is dead."

He looked up at the portrait of Lorrie King, put his face in his hands.

"Oh God," he said. "Oh Jesus."

I waited. After a long time he began to get rid of it, haltingly, in those driven, throat-clogged tones he had used the first time I'd seen him.

"Lorrie called me," he said. "It was a Sunday afternoon. I'd only known her a short time—I loved her—already I was gone for her. She sounded desperate. I went to her apartment and she was there with the girl—

Russo? But she had the girl in the bedroom, the door closed. I never saw her while I was there. She never saw me. Lorrie had thought of that.

"She told me about it. The girl was hysterical, determined not to have the baby. Her brother, some wild Italian kid, was going to shoot up the neighborhood. The girl had already tried to abort herself. Lorrie asked me—if there was anything I could do. And I said if she asked me to I'd jump off the goddam roof! I said yes. In my office."

He pushed himself to his feet, went for another drink of water and came back.

"Did you explain to Miss King that she would be an accomplice?" I asked.

"Of course. I explained everything. She wasn't interested in that. She would protect me and that was all she cared. Just so the girl wouldn't flip."

He pushed back his hair roughly.

"So I went to the office and Lorrie brought the girl— and she let her look around at the place, but then she put the blindfold on her and stayed with her. There wasn't much to the treatment. The girl hadn't injured herself and she wasn't far along. It was safe and everything went all right. And Lorrie took her away as soon as it was possible. She never saw me or heard my name. Until tonight."

He had been standing, half turned from me, looking up now and then over his shoulder at the portrait. Suddenly he whirled, bent at the waist as if seized by cramps, and his eyes bored up at me.

"You said—there was evidence of this— blackmail before! Another victim."

I braced myself and kept quiet.

"Who?" he said. His voice rose in that thin, strident scream. "Who was it? It was Lorrie!"

"Yes," I said.

He was shaking all over. His hands made pale fists. His mouth was distorted.

"Lorrie!" he said.

"Over a period of two years," I said. "That's what those little memos were about. I think she saved them with some vague idea of turning him in some time. But she never did."

"Because of me," he said, falling away from me toward the bed. "She took it—from that dirty cop."

He came up again, flying at me. I caught his arms and eased him off a little, hanging on till he stopped shaking.

"I had him right there, isolated, just the two of us. Saunders. I would have killed him—!"

He pulled free of me and stood with his back to the portrait, his shoulders hunched like those of a fighter coming out of his corner.

"I'm sure you would have," I said. "But that's not the way it goes. Besides, there was the girl."

"Saunders drove her to it," he said. "Saunders was the one."

I glanced up at the portrait and looked away from it.

"She had many pressures on her," I said. "Saunders was only part of it. She had the Russo boy in a rage for her. The Russo boy died five days ago, the day before Lorrie—Miss King . . . There was Dillon, dependent on her for moral courage and money. There was Edward Rounds, who had wanted to marry her and had given her a bad time with his stuffy, niggling self-righteousness. But he couldn't forget her and he was starting to bug her again within the last few weeks. To the extent that his wife put a private eye on him, and then he—but the hell with that. It's all over now. And then," I went on, "there was you."

He turned slowly, staring at me.

"You were demanding," I said. "Maybe you didn't realize it, but you demanded a lot of her. That she break with Dillon. You wanted to change her, her attitudes, you called them. That's the same as changing her way of life. You thought in a certain way and you wanted her to think the same."

"No—!"

"And you let her carry that thing about the abortion —alone."

"I didn't know Saunders—"

"Aside from Saunders," I said. "You might have got her off that hook, but you had to protect yourself, and your career. I suppose that's inescapable. You must be conditioned that way."

He stared at me for a long time, then his eyes lifted to the portrait. They closed, opened again, blinking, and he turned and threw himself face down on the bed. I waited a short time, but he stayed where he was and I took one last look at the portrait of Lorrie King and said good night.

"Try and get some sleep," I said. "I'll help you through Saunders' trial, if you want me."

He didn't say anything. I backed out of the room and let myself out and went downstairs to find another taxi.

There was no light showing under Byron Dillon's door, but I rang anyway. Nobody came. I gave it enough time and went back to the street. Two doors down, soft light glowed in the canopied doorway of a neighborhood cocktail lounge. I took a seat at the bar and ordered a drink. The place was nearly deserted. A few stools down from me sat a middle-aged couple. There were no other customers.

The bartender was one to mind his own business, but when I ordered the second drink, he stayed long enough to catch my question.

"Dillon? The artist?" he said. "Sure. He's in here sometimes."

"Have you seen him tonight?"

The bartender thought it over, made a thing with his mouth and shook his head.

"Not tonight," he said.

"Have any idea where he might be? Any special hang-out?"

He gave me a look, shrugged and went away. I finished my drink and he came back. I pushed a two-dollar tip across the bar.

"Might try the Black Knight, on Chicago," he said.

"Thanks," I said and got down.

It was after ten now. The rain had stopped. The streets were wet and shiny in the light, but the air was fresh and not too cold. I walked over to Chicago Avenue and down past Rush Street to the Black Knight.

It was larger and more pretentious than the previous spa and doing a good business. I had never seen it inside. I had avoided it as a known homosexual hangout. I felt uneasy now as I found a vacant stool at the bar and ordered a drink. After about five minutes, though, I got over it. Nobody paid any attention to me. There were a few women in the place, but most of the customers were male. I couldn't tell at a glance whether the women were male or female.

There was a good deal of traffic in and out, but Dillon wasn't part of it. I sat for a long time, wondering how to raise my questions. Seldom before, anywhere, had I felt such a stranger.

One of the bartenders frowned at my half-empty glass. Pretty soon he frowned again. A fellow sat down on the stool to my left. I avoided looking at him. The bartender brought him a drink and I found my nerve.

"You acquainted with Byron Dillon, the artist?" I asked.

"Yes," the bartender said, "I am."

He started away.

"Hey, Brown-eyes," the one next to me called.

The bartender came back, frowning.

"The man wants to ask you about Byron Dillon," the fellow said.

I looked at him then. He was a guy I knew slightly, a cop on the vice squad named George Plummer. We didn't acknowledge each other. Brown-eyes glared at him, then condescended to look at me.

"What did you wish to ask?" he said.

"Well—" I said, "I'd like to talk to Dillon—about a

picture of his—and I can't find him. Somebody suggested I look in here."

The bartender appeared to survey the room. It didn't take long.

"He's not here," he said.

"Has he been here?"

"I believe so. Earlier."

"About how much earlier?"

He shrugged.

"Maybe an hour."

"Do you have any suggestions where I might look for him?"

The bartender looked at the man next to me.

"Are you together?" he asked.

"No," he said. "Answer the question, Brown-eyes."

The bartender's face was a study in suppressed rage.

"You might try the Golden Cock," he said. "He has some of his work hanging there."

"Thank you," I said.

He walked away down the bar.

"Hello, George," I said.

"Hi, Mac."

"Thanks for the lift."

"Forget it. You got to be tough with these people. They're so goddam uppity."

I had no great love or respect for the vice squad, but I had always gotten along all right with George.

"I wouldn't know," I said.

"What do you want with Dillon?"

I shrugged.

"Is it a vice matter?"

"No," I said.

"All right," he said. "Dillon's not a bad guy. He stays out of trouble."

"I'm glad to hear it," I said.

"If you go to the Golden Cock," he said, "there's a piano player named Barney. He's all right, if you need help."

"Thanks again. Where is the joint?"

"Few blocks north, on Clark Street."

"Yeah, I've seen it. So long, George."

"Good luck," he said.

I went out and did some more walking.

The place was smaller and less elegant than the Black Knight and showed traces of the old Bohemian atmosphere of the neighborhood—not very authentic traces. Paintings hung in a dimly lighted foyer. I noticed several by Dillon. The other signatures meant nothing to me. Inside I could hear the music, a solid, noncontroversial piano.

There were deep leather booths along the walls, and a somewhat posh bar, long and curving, of finely wrought mahogany. Over the backbar hung a blown-up print of the *Naked Maja*. The satire was broad and tasteless.

Barney the piano player was a Negro, bulky and beaming. The piano bar was filled and I found a stool facing the naked lady and ordered a slug of bourbon. As at the Black Knight, nobody took any notice of me, but the service was more brisk and a little more courteous.

I guess I look like a cop, I thought. I guess there's no disguise.

It took me a long time to check every person in the place and I had to take a trip to the men's room in order to cover a rear corner beyond the bar. By then I was satisfied that Byron Dillon wasn't present.

I waited about fifteen minutes and a seat opened at the piano bar, near the keyboard. I took my drink over there and sat down. Barney finished a tune, sipped at a tall, dark-brown glass and wrinkled his face at me.

"Yeah, dad," he said. "What do you like?"

I got out a dollar bill and dropped it in his kitty.

"Whatever you like," I said.

"Way I like it," he said moodily and pretty soon began playing again.

He played well. He had good hands for it and he knew where the music was. It was after eleven now and I was tired and without expectations. It would have been pleasant to sit there with the music until closing time and then go home to bed.

When Barney finished his long drink, I bought him another. There was some turnover around the piano and I inspected each new face, but Dillon didn't appear.

Barney lifted his glass to me and I nodded.

"Want something?" he murmured, bending low over the keyboard.

"George Plummer," I said, "told me you could help."

"Cop," he mused. "Who's in trouble, man?"

"Nobody," I said. "I want to talk to Byron Dillon."

"Artist man," he said.

"Yeah."

He played some moody, slow piece that he must have improvised. It was always on the verge of being recognizable, but never quite made it.

"Man got grief," he said out of nowhere.

"Dillon?" I said.

He nodded over the keys, searched, found what he wanted.

"He was here?" I said.

"Yeah, he was here. Gone."

"Will he be back?"

He grinned at me out of his crinkly face.

"You tell me," he said. "Tell me, man."

"Where will I look?" I asked.

He shrugged and wrinkled his face as if in thought. After a while he said,

"Some place dark," he said. "Head for the river."

"On the Street?"

"West, man," he murmured. "Go west—Old Town and then some."

It was raining again, but lightly. West of Clark, beyond Halstead, I went at it systematically, crisscrossing the street, into this tavern, out and into that joint across the street, and back and forth. I was no longer in fairyland and it was hard to believe that Dillon would frequent these brassy bistros.

I no longer bought drinks or bothered the bartenders. I just walked in, looked for him and went on to the next spot. It was an off night, so they weren't crowded, and it didn't take long to check them out.

With only two of them left between me and the river, I was forced into asking questions. It had begun to look as if Barney had guessed wrong, or if he hadn't, that I had been less than thorough.

The two spots were across the street from each other. I flipped a coin, it came up heads and I crossed the street. Business was far off and nothing was going on except a neighborhood bull session in a rear booth. One man drowsed over a glass of beer at the bar. I sat down there and ordered one for myself. The bartender didn't know Byron Dillon by name or reputation. He pointed to the booth in the back.

"Maybe one of them knows," he said. "There's a couple of commercial artists back there."

I took my glass and wandered back there. Two of the seven in the big booth were playing gin rummy. The others were bulling it up. I stood watching the game and after a while one of them looked up at me.

"Hi," he said.

"I'm looking for Byron Dillon," I said.

There was some silence. The game went on at the same pace. Somebody said,

"Dillon."

Another looked at me.

"What do you want with him?"

"Just to talk."

They looked at each other for a while.

"He was in here," somebody said. "He left. He got invited."

Somebody laughed.

"I wish it was me invited," he said.

They had sparked each other.

"He's drowning in his own goddam faggot tears," a fellow said. "His girl left him."

"His girl?" I said.

"His wife. His friend."

"How long has he been gone?" I asked. "Dillon."

There was some general shrugging.

"You know how it is with time," one said.

"Maybe twenty minutes," another said.

I started away.

"Might try across the street," somebody called. "That's the last stop before the river."

An urgency persisted after the joke had faded. Out on the street I looked across at the "last chance" saloon. Dingier than any of the others from the outside, it seemed to lean slightly. But this was a trick of the light against the ragged neon over the door. It was called The Launching Pad, but a couple of the letters had gone out and it gave the façade a tentative look.

Inside a shaggy bartender shook his head when I mentioned Dillon's name.

"Police stuff?" he said.

"No," I said.

"Fella went out of here about five, ten minutes ago. Could hardly walk. I couldn't serve him."

"Did you see which way he went?"

"Hell no. For all I know he went straight up—or down."

I went out into the rain and looked over the street.

The lights straggled away to my right. To my left it sloped briefly to a low wall and beyond that was the river. I walked that way slowly. By now my jacket was well soaked and hung heavily on my shoulders. My hat brim had drooped and I had to carry my face tilted upward in order to see.

At the wall I lingered for a few minutes, then went along it, east, toward Halstead. There was a strong odor of wet oil and sewer gas from the river, and looking across, I could see the sweeping lights of the desultory traffic on the expressway.

About half a block from the foot of the street I had just left, a man was lying crumpled in a recessed doorway, the only visible break in a solid brick wall. I leaned over him, lit a match and it was Dillon. I tossed the match away and set to waking him up.

It took some time. He was saturated with drink; it was a sour, enveloping aroma. His head lolled helplessly when I shook him. I got my arms under his and dragged him up till he was sitting against the door. I pushed his head back some and let the rain wash his face. After a while he blinked and took some notice.

"Dillon—" I said. "Come on. I'll take you home."

He grunted something and tried to go back to sleep. I slapped one side of his face lightly, then the other, and brought him back. This time he looked at me and pushed back fearfully.

"Who?" he said.

"Mac," I said. "Come on now. I'll help you up. We'll get a cab."

"Leave me alone."

I got a firm grip on his jacket under his arms and lifted him. He came to his feet, sagged against me, then against the wall. I held him till he steadied, then led him back toward the street, toward that last saloon, where I could call a cab.

17

THE DRIVER had to help me get him into his apartment. We put him on the studio couch and the driver went away. I took off my jacket and the holster and gun I had been wearing under it, draped the coat over the holster and sat down in a chair to wait until he could communicate.

I fell asleep and woke, chilled. I went to the kitchen, drew a glass of hot water and drank it. The kitchen was disorderly, with a pile of dirty dishes on the sinkboard, a towel on the floor. I picked up the towel and left the dishes. I walked around, swinging my arms to get the circulation going, and Dillon began to stir. But he didn't quite make it and I sat down again.

There was the sound of a key in the apartment door. I sat where I was. The door opened and Frankie, Dillon's friend, came in. He was wearing a lightweight trench coat and no hat and his longish blond hair was wet with rain.

He stopped abruptly when he saw me in the chair. Then he glanced at Dillon's sprawled figure on the couch, closed the door quietly and leaned against it.

"Drunk?" he said.

I nodded.

He went to the couch, stood looking down at Dillon for a while, then turned away.

"What do you want with him?" he asked.

I shrugged.

"I brought him home."

"Oh. That was—nice of you."

He looked at Dillon again.

"I—walked out on him," he said. "It became impossible."

"I'm sorry," I said. "Any specific reason?"

His eyes withdrew.

"No," he said, "just an accumulation of—things."

"How long have you been gone?"

"Since early last evening."

There was a silence. Dillon was on his back now and had begun to snore. He was badly disheveled and needed a shave.

"Well, thanks for helping him home," Frankie said. "I'll stay until he's all right. You probably want to get away."

"I have to talk to him," I said.

He looked at me for quite a long time, then shrugged, took off his coat and started away.

"I'll make a pot of coffee," he said.

"That would be pleasant," I said, "but don't do it for me."

"He'll need it when he wakes up," Frankie said.

He went to the kitchen and I heard him making the coffee. Evidently we had disturbed Dillon. He was restless. I heard him groan, watched him roll over and put both hands to his head. Gradually he woke, taking no notice of me or anything that I could see in the room. He forced his legs over the side, pushed up on both hands and, leaning, shook his head, then halted abruptly. He was shaggy and damp and his jacket hung awry from his higher shoulder. At length, squeezing his eyes open and shut and open again, he looked at me.

"You," he said.

His voice was thick and distant in his throat.

"Hello," I said.

He sat up, squirmed in his jacket, pulled his tie loose and managed to loosen his collar.

"You're that—cop," he said.

"The private one."

He looked far off into space, as if trying to comprehend.

"Where in hell have I been?" he said.

"Here and there."

He belched.

"Here and there—? For two days? Here and there?"

"I don't know. I just found you about an hour ago."

Another belch.

"Okay," he said. Then, "Where? Where—you find me?"

"Down by the river."

"Down by the river—side," he said. "Down by the goddam riverside."

"Yeah," I said.

"Frankie—" he said. "Frankie left me."

"Frankie's here now," I said. "He's making some coffee."

"He's—what?"

"He's here—"

"Oh no. Not here. He wouldn't dare."

I had said the wrong thing about Frankie.

"Because—" Dillon said, his mouth working over it, "Frankie is a—rat fink."

"All right," I said.

Excuse me, Frankie, I thought.

"What do you want?" he said.

"I want a few words with you, when you feel like it."

"When I feel like—it—"

Frankie came in with a coffeepot and some piled-up cups and saucers. When he saw that Dillon was sitting up, he hesitated, then set everything down on a table some distance away. Dillon appeared at first not to recognize him. Warily, Frankie poured coffee, nodded to me. I picked up a cup and started in on it, feeling the good heat of it in my wet bones. After a minute, Frankie filled another cup and carried it to the couch.

Dillon appeared to be blind. He put his face in his hands, rubbed it roughly, looked up. Frankie was standing patiently, holding the saucer with the steaming cup. Dillon's face twisted; his eyes widened with recognition. Without warning, he lashed upward with his right hand. Frankie screamed as the near-boiling coffee splashed into his face, ran down his shirt. I set my own cup on the table, but before I could reach them, Dillon was on his feet.

It was no fit of pique. Dillon was out to kill. His fists battered at Frankie's face and head. The smaller one, no fighter to begin with, had his hands up, trying to protect himself. There was an ugly reddening of the skin of his face and neck where the coffee had burned him.

I got both arms around Dillon, holding him momentarily, pinning him back. But he was in a rage and strong

181

and he broke away quickly. Frankie had fallen in a help-less crouch, his head in his arms, and Dillon eluded me and kicked at his ribs and flanks. I grabbed Dillon again, awkwardly, by one arm and a shred of his jacket and swung him away toward the couch. Frankie was getting up. I tried to help him, but he broke away and ran from the room. Dillon plunged after him. I managed to deflect him with my shoulder and he reeled and fell against the wall, dragging a window curtain down with him. The rod fell and the heavy drapery folds enveloped him.

I leaned down to uncover and disentangle him and he came charging up blindly, unexpectedly, and his head by a freak stroke hit me in the chin like a batted ball. I fought the battle to stay awake and lost. I was out only for moments, but when I could see, Dillon had got free of the drape and was plunging out of the room. I made it to my feet and went after him. There was a bedroom. I caught sight of Frankie stretched face down on a rumpled satin spread. Beyond a door opened on Dillon's studio. As I reached it, it slammed in my face. The noise was shattering and it brought Frankie into a crouch on the bed.

"You going to be all right?" I asked.

He just shook his head, staring at the closed studio door. From inside I could hear sounds of destruction, banging and ripping.

"Oh no—" Frankie said. "Oh God no!"

I got the door open. In the dimly lighted studio I could see Dillon destroying his work—tearing pictures from the walls, smashing the glass in the frames, ripping out canvases, crumpling and throwing them away wildly. Canvases were stacked against the wall and he kicked at them, trampled them.

In the center of the room, on a large easel, was the portrait of a woman, barely begun, a blond woman— Lorrie King. As I recognized it, Dillon flew at it. He had found a knife and attacked the portrait viciously, stabbing and cutting at it, despoiling the face, the hair, the shoulders.

I felt a nudge and Frankie forced his way past me into the studio. His voice rose in that scream of pain, as when he had been hit by the coffee.

"Byron! No—! Please—no!"

Dillon paid no attention.

"Stop him!" Frankie screamed at me.

I doubted that I could stop him without somebody getting hurt—him with that knife.

"Stay out of the way," I said.

Dillon was still hacking at the portrait when I moved in behind him, wary of the knife in his right hand. I got both hands on his wrist, but he jerked free and slashed at me once. Ducking, I tripped and he kicked at me. I came up under his arm and got the wrist again and this time I hung on. But I was off balance and he swung on me, a blow on the head that drove me to my knees. I twisted his arm then and whipped him around to bring him down to my level. He gave up under the pressure and dropped the knife, but he was still fighting. I hit him under the ribs once and once in the jaw and he quit, rolling onto his side on the floor. Frankie ran to him, knelt and tried to help him up, but Dillon pushed him away, cursing, got to his feet and stumbled into the bedroom.

My forearm was wet under my shirt and I pushed up the sleeve and found he had cut me between the wrist and elbow, inside. I wrapped my handkerchief around it. Frankie, from a weird, unaware crouch, stared at me, then looked toward the bedroom. I sat on the floor for a minute, then got up and made my way to the wall and leaned there.

"Byron?" Frankie called.

After a minute, Dillon appeared in the doorway, wiping his face with his hands. His voice was hoarse and deep in his throat.

"What do you want from me?" he said.

"Just talk to me," I said. "About Lorrie King, and about what happened the night she died."

He leaned on the doorjamb with his face against his arm. Then he looked up and he talked. It came out rough and sticky, like spitting out bits of cotton candy.

"It was—" he said. "I didn't set out to—kill her. Who would destroy her—so beautiful! It was that—it just began to happen and I couldn't stop. I kept thinking of that goddam—doctor! Seeing her in that life—" He pushed himself from the door. "I was trying to—*save* her!"

He moved unevenly toward the devastated portrait hanging in shreds on the easel. Frankie, still crouching, watched out of his burned face.

It must hurt like hell, I thought.

"How did it start?" I asked.

Dillon began to talk again, as if to some remote, unseen listener.

"She was tired—she said she hadn't slept for three days. There was something about some boy, some Italian kid, who got killed in a street brawl. She blamed herself. She took everything on herself.

"I said I would leave and she said no, stay, she only wanted to get to bed. She asked if I'd read to her.

"And so—I went in the bedroom and she was in bed. There was a bottle of pills on the stand—Seconal, I think. She said, 'I took two, do you think that's all right?' And I said I thought so. And I began reading to her—some poems, modern—I don't remember who wrote them.

"I read about three of them and she fell asleep. I had just noticed that—and the goddam telephone rang. It woke her—I thought she'd jump clear out of bed—and it was the good doctor.

"So I left the room and he kept her on the goddam phone for half an hour. I didn't try to listen. When I went back, she was upset, crying. I asked if she wanted me to read any more and she just got out of bed, picked up the bottle of pills and went to the bathroom. I don't know how many of the pills were left—not many, I think.

"I waited a long time—I started to leave, then came back. I had heard water running, then it was quiet. I waited about forty-five minutes, I think, and then I got worried and knocked on the door and there wasn't any answer. So I looked and she was in the tub, sound asleep. The pill bottle was on the lavatory—empty.

"At first, I thought I would wake her up and get her back to bed. The water was cool and there was gooseflesh on her neck and shoulders. She was lying against the—you know—curve of the tub, with her legs straight out. She was so lovely—so peaceful. I got down on my knees beside the tub and just looked at her, and I thought of her with that damn doctor, and of the Italian kid, and—I can't explain what happened. Something happened. Like a fog, when a fog comes in and you keep trying to see through it and little by little everything is blocked out, except the nearest things, and all I could see was Lorrie, at peace, always, and I was hating the doctor at the same time. 'He would kill you, Lorrie,' I thought. I think I said it out loud.

"Anyway, I wasn't thinking any more, just acting—I opened the medicine chest and took out a razor blade and I cut the veins in her wrists—tiny blue veins—very quickly, once each. She winced and her eyes opened, but she was very groggy. I patted her shoulder and said something to her and she closed her eyes and her wrists were bleeding in the water in the tub. And then I raised her knees and slid her down at the shoulders—she had been lying against that porcelain, or whatever it is, and she stuck to it a little. But I raised her knees and she slid down and I turned her head and pushed a little more and her nose went under—and I held her there—it only took a couple of minutes. She struggled a little bit, but not much—I don't think she ever knew what was happening—"